Readers Love RHYS FORD

Back in Black

"Even if you haven't read any of the other books in the series…get them all, including this one. You won't be sorry"

—Sparking Book Reviews

Ramen Assassin

"Suspense and mystery mixed with romance and characters that are so well written, you feel like you've known them for years."

—Diverse Reader

Rebel

"I loved the writing , loved the banter and loved all the various characters. ALL of them."

—Santy's Bookshelf

Sinner's Gin

"This was my first by Rhys Ford. It obviously will not be my last. I highly recommend this."

—On Top Down Under Book Reviews

Dirty Kiss

"…Ford has definitely found her niche' with murder, mayhem and snarky, sexy, half-naked men that can't seem to keep their hands off of each other."

—MM Good Book Reviews

By Rhys Ford

Published by DREAMSPINNER PRESS
www.dreamspinnerpress.com

RHYS FORD

PORT IN A STORM

Published by
DREAMSPINNER PRESS

8219 Woodville Hwy #1245
Woodville, FL 32362 USA
www.dreamspinnerpress.com

This is a work of fiction. Names, characters, places, and incidents either are the product of author imagination or are used fictitiously, and any resemblance to actual persons, living or dead, business establishments, events, or locales is entirely coincidental.

Port in a Storm
© 2024 Rhys Ford

Cover Art
© 2023 Cover Art by Reece Notley
reece@vitaenoir.com
Cover content is for illustrative purposes only and any person depicted on the cover is a model.

Mass Market Paperback ISBN: 978-1-64405-578-6
Trade Paperback ISBN: 978-1-64405-848-0
Digital ISBN: 978-1-64405-847-3
Trade Paperback published January 2023
v. 1.0

Printed in the United States of America
∞
This paper meets the requirements of
ANSI/NISO Z39.48-1992 (Permanence of Paper).

DEDICATION

As always, this book is dedicated to the Five—Penny, Lea, Tamm, and our sister who was off causing chaos in the cosmos, Jenn. I am forever grateful for having all of you to stitch me together when I begin to unravel and to yank at my chain when I go astray.

I also want to send my love to Bru, Mink, and Michelle, who have kept me company as I walk along the edge of all of my cliffs.

Lastly, my darling Gus... Dude's Inspiration aka The Potato, Genghis Cairn, and the star of the Borking Report... You are so very dearly missed, my blond grumpy ottoman. I wish you could've stayed with me a little bit longer, but I understand your need to frolic across the rainbow bridge and join your brothers. Please send them all my love, and for fuck's sake, don't bork at the gardeners. They are just trying to do their jobs.

ACKNOWLEDGMENTS

First and foremost, I have to extend a deeply felt thank-you for everyone in my Coffee, Cats, and Murder group on Facebook. They have continued to support me and encourage me over a brutal few years, and I wouldn't have returned to the keyboard without their daily chatter and cat memes.

I would also like to thank Elizabeth North, Naomi Grant, Gin, Liz, and Brian for sticking with me as I hammered out this novel. It was a pleasure to return to the *Sinners* world one last time and bring to life a story I knew I had to write, if only to get it out of my head.

And lastly, Badger, Harley, and Gojira deserve a shout-out because they each kept my lap and left knee warm while I wrote.

CHAPTER ONE

THE KID'S eyes were the color of fiery anguish poured into crystal blue waters, a shimmering shift of pain and fear clouded by tears and thick lashes stuck together by grime. Standing in the middle of a cloud of dissipating tear gas, he—maybe she—shook when Lt. Connor Morgan's light beam swept through the trash-filled room.

Not something Connor expected when he strapped his body armor on that afternoon. Sure as hell not where he ever thought his life would lead him to… standing in front of a frightened little kid who smelled of piss and fear.

Back at the station the raid scoped out like any other—breaking down doors and rousting whoever they found in the hopes of finding someone to connect the SFPD to a well-known and even more well-hidden drug dealer. On paper everything looked routine, but Connor and his team had rapped open enough doors to know the job was never routine, and this one was no exception.

This one sure as hell kicked them all in the balls.

The house wasn't much to talk about from the curb, unless of course it was one of the neighbors who bemoaned the abandoned rusting car parked in the weeds growing up through missing fenders and floorboards or complained to the city about the overturned trash bins spilling out used syringes and rotting food onto the broken cement driveway. At one point, the tiny cottage had boasted a bright blue coat of paint and cream gingerbread trim, but that was before time, neglect, and harsh weather had a chance to pick away at its frame. Half of its roof was missing shingles, leaving black tar paper flapping about when the wind picked up, and its few screens hung off-kilter on mostly broken windows.

Even with his face mask in place, Connor smelled the rot and mold as soon as they hit the porch, his team ducking down to avoid catching their equipment on the sagging overhang above their heads. A battering ram made quick work of a frail front door, the blasting boom of the leads coordinated with the second team's breach of the back entrance.

They'd gone in quietly, as swiftly as shadows moving across a grassy lawn on a hot midsummer day. Briefed on their target, each team member had memorized the sneering face they'd been presented with, but there were other unknowns to consider, especially since the house was a known buy-and-use spot. Bullets weren't the only thing they had to worry about—a stray needle prick brought its own horrific troubles, and every cop going through the doors that evening was well aware of the consequences of one wrong step. Steel or lead could bring them down, either quickly or slowly, but death was a grim certainty if something got through their heavy combat boots and body armor.

That wasn't the way Connor wanted to go out. And it sure as hell wasn't going to be how he'd ever lose a team member. He'd told his squad time and time again that retiring out was the only acceptable way to hang up their SWAT designation, yet at every briefing, he studied his team's faces, knowing it could very well be the last time.

Every time Connor went through the door, he reminded his team to stay safe. Everyone had people waiting for them to come home, and he was no exception. He saw the worry in Forest's soulful eyes every time they kissed each other before Connor left for work. The same look his mother often had when his father and any of her children who also wore an SFPD star walked out of the front door. There was always a slight chance the next cop on the stoop would be wearing a dress uniform, hat in hand and words of deep sympathy on their tongues. He never wanted to wear another piece of black tape on his star ever again, and he sure as hell didn't want one worn for him.

He'd gone in hot, weapon raised and leading the charge with a couple of other senior cops, ducking around the ram to burst into the cramped front hall. A rolling canister of gas hit the stained carpet clumped up over the living room floor, and from there, they began their assault.

"Left cleared!"

The rattle of thin floorboards being hammered by heavy boots partially muted the screaming coming from somewhere in the back of the house. Smoke from shield grenades shifted the air from dank to milky, the swirling ghostly fronds grabbing at the illumination spots on the ends of the team's weapons. Connor's team cut through the choking gases, their faces obscured by masks and goggles, but he knew them well enough to

ID who moved around him, skulking through the decrepit, abandoned house to clear the way for the retention team that followed them in.

Broken furniture and rusted appliances gathered at the edges of the main room, much like seafoam and flotsam brought in by an erratic tide. Several stained mattresses lay on the floor, cheap fleece throws bunched up between them. The acrid scent of cooking drugs was probably being drowned out by the tear gas they'd used after breaching the front door, but Connor could only smell the faint metallic tang of the filtered air he was pulling into his lungs. A bout of coughing alerted them to their first suspect—a skinny, scab-encrusted young man with wild eyes. Hansen grabbed him before he could bolt, the junior member of the team working the protesting teen's hands into a pair of crisscrossed zip ties to immobilize him.

"Leave him for the perimeter guys," Connor ordered. "Let's get the house clear."

It was a textbook takedown, scattering the squatters in the front of the house like cockroaches under a bright light. Connor's team followed the screaming as they hunted through the shadows for any of the faces they'd been briefed on. At first glance, the dilapidated property's cramped rooms didn't look large enough to hold more than five people at a time, but every single SWAT member knew appearances could be deceiving. There were bolt holes in the walls, drywall barriers set up along spaces that should have been hallways. The blueprints they'd studied before going in were wildly inaccurate—giant holes punched through old plaster in some places and a tangle of barbed wire and steel plates blocking what should have been open doorways.

Connor slowed his team down, pulling back slightly in order to give everyone time to adjust to the reconfigured layout. On his right side, Yamamoto gave the all-clear to enter through the door ahead of them, throwing up a hand signal and motioning the backup team forward. To Connor's left was a gaping maw where a wall should have been, and he covered the opening as the two-man crew hustled past. Someone shouted—probably Yamamoto—and another gas canister rolled down the hallway, obscuring progress of the advancing teams.

Even as hastily put together as the operation was, they knew who they were looking for. The DA and their captain kept their division hot on the trail of a drug dealer named Robinson, and a few hours ago, someone's informant gave good intel about the slippery criminal's intentions of shaking loose the squatters so he could use the property to cook up meth to supply his pipeline. Concentrating on breaking his supply chain, Connor and the other SWAT leaders coordinated their strikes, pulling in as many resources as they could to support the multi-pronged offensive. It'd been a long month, and this was his team's third pop-up raid in two weeks, with little time between them to plan.

The aggressive tactics orchestrated by the district attorney and the San Francisco Police Department appeared to be working, because Robinson seemed to be scrambling, working his way outward to locations far beyond his normal stomping grounds and into territories already held by other crime factions. It seemed lately the best way for someone to get rid of their competitor was simply a phone call to the cops, choosing to let the SFPD take them out rather than enter into a bloody war.

Whoever it was that dropped that dime would have his own reckoning sometime soon, but for today, he was safe in the shadows. As Yamamoto often said, they had bigger roaches to pin down.

"Morgan, I've got a runner in the back," a voice Connor recognized as another SWAT team leader rumbled through his earpiece. "Might be Robinson. My team's going to follow for backup."

"Typical Grady, always hogging the spotlight," Yamamoto teased over the mic. "Alpha C, continue to sweep."

"Watch your backs," Connor warned his team members over the line. "We don't know who Robinson brought with him and what they're carrying. Yama, cover me. I'm going to take the first room."

"Got your back." Yamamoto stepped in tight against the opening. Putting his weapon up and his back against the wall, the cop nodded at Connor. "On your go."

Turning toward the small bedroom visible only through the hole in the wall, Connor pulled up as soon as he spotted the kid.

Those damned eyes held him, trapping Con in midstep. Shocked wide but filled with pain and resignation, the child couldn't have been much more than five, but it was as hard to tell as trying to figure out its gender. Scrawny to the point of bony, he trembled when Connor ducked his head down to enter the room. Keeping the kid in view as he swept the room wasn't hard. The area was little more than a closet, walled off from the rest of a larger space by a few braced drywall sheets and heavy dinged-up bookcases.

None of them ever expected to find a kid, but no one was surprised either. Or at least Con wasn't. Not now. Not after finding so many tiny bodies nested in the filth shored up around society's edges. And here the boy was. Or at least, up close, the kid looked more like a boy. Only time would tell.

"Morgan—" Yamamoto's shout was cut off, staggered bits of sound sliced in between rapid pops of gunfire.

Something hot and hard struck Connor's shoulder, pushing him farther into the room. The kid peeled his mouth open, chipped front teeth cutting at his upper lip when he let loose a terrified yowl. Like Yamamoto's warning, the shrill fear-driven siren murmured beneath the louder screams of a hail of smoking bullets tearing into the hall's walls, and Connor leaped forward, hooked one arm around the boy's skinny torso, and pulled him down.

The bite of fear grabbed at Connor's throat, and he tamped away the flickering embers before they could catch hold. Facedown in a scatter of debris, he held the boy against him, chin to his chest, hoping his SWAT armor would be enough to stop anything from piercing the kid's body. The punch of bullets through the wall stretched out, elongating seconds, and Con sucked in some air, tasting the filth of the room even through his mask.

It wasn't until he moved his head to the right that he saw the dead woman lying half hidden under a pile of grimy blankets, her white, glazed eyes fixedly staring at some point in the universe only she could see, her slack lips speckled with blood and dried fly shit. Long knotted chunks of hair obscured a good part of her face, bits of blue dye faded to a dull aquamarine at the ends. Buried beneath the trash, he hadn't seen her when he'd come into the room, but lying on the ground, protecting the kid from gunfire gave Connor a very clear view of where she'd taken her last breath.

It was hard to tell how long she'd been dead. Her flesh stretched tight across her cheekbones and pointy chin, but the smeared mascara around her dulled dun-colored eyes could have hidden a number of sins and years. Her face, savaged by addiction and split-open sores, was as gray as the thin mattress she lay on. Her left hand poked out from under a crumpled blue tarp that covered the rest of her body. She'd been caught in the throes of a seizure, or maybe she'd been reaching for something or even someone, like the kid, but death grabbed her before she could grasp what she wanted. Her broken nails were as filthy as the boy's face, and her skeletal fingers were clenched at the empty air, cheap silver rings rattling around her bony knuckles.

Another booming blast shook the house.

"Keep your head down, kid," Connor growled when the boy began to squirm. If anything, the fray and shouting in the rest of the house seemed to intensify. "Yama, give me a status."

"Pinned down at the end of the hall, sir," the man's voice crackled over the headset. "You okay? Who ya' talking to?"

"Got a little boy—I think—here. Anywhere clear to get him out?" Pain flared in Connor's shoulder when he moved. The child's weight pulled down on his muscles, straining the tender spots blooming on his back. He'd either landed in something wet or the hits he'd taken were more serious than he thought.

"Negative, but I can give you cover," Yamamoto said over the comm. "Working back down the hall. Can you hold?"

"Holding." Connor wrapped his arms around the boy's torso, trying to cover as much as possible. "Get your arms down, kiddo, and grab anything you can on my vest."

The child was rigid, legs stick straight and stiff. His tiny hands were dotted with bruises and dried blood, his knuckles bleached white when his fingers tightened around the straps on Connor's armor. He buried his face into Connor's chest, breathing hard and heavy when another round of gunfire opened up in the hall.

A pair of large dark shadows fell across the opening in the wall, and then Yamamoto angled his back against one side of the broken drywall. He gave Connor a hand signal, then counted down from three to a closed fist and began a heavy barrage of sprayed shots. Gun drawn, Connor ducked out to the right, keeping the boy against his chest. He moved quickly, pausing at openings and long stretches of the hallway, alert to any movement.

When his boots hit the living room floor, Yamamoto gave the all-clear to move the fight to the back of the house again, leaving Connor with an easier egress. The young man they'd left for the other team was gone, hopefully safe and sound away from the raid. The pain along Connor's shoulders was turning from a dull throb to a raging fire, and as he tried to clear the mound of debris, he stumbled and caught the tip of his boot on something hard. The kid let out a short yelp of terror when Connor's grasp loosened. Then he sobbed brokenly as Connor tightened his grip.

"I'm not going to drop you," he reassured the little boy. "I've got you. You're safe."

The front door seemed miles away, the small house telescoping outward with each report of gunfire. Keeping down, Connor shouted his egress to the team members waiting outside. The canister smoke thickened as he ran, making the little boy cough with each breath. He burst through the off-kilter screen door, breaking the hinges with the force of his shoulder against the wobbly metal frame. The air outside wasn't any clearer, but Connor shoved his gun into its holster then removed his mask while he ran toward the SWAT vehicles parked along the opposite curb. Pressing the plastic cup over the boy's face, he picked up speed, trying to get them clear of the house and the raging gunfight.

Promises weighed heavy on Connor's shoulders—promises to come home, promises he'd keep someone safe. He felt every word he'd turned into a vow piercing his soul with each pounding stride he took and the boy's scared, rigid body trembling against his chest.

The comm chatter was a distraction, giving Connor a good idea of what was behind him. Children out first. That was how they operated, what the team swore to do on each raid. Another promise he'd made, despite the fear he was leaving his people behind to die. Yamamoto was good. Hell, the other team was nearly as good as his own. He should have had nothing to worry about, but dread crept in, wiggling past his defenses and eating away at the idea that everyone who answered to him would walk out of that door on their own.

The strobing blue-and-red lights flashed over the rain-damp asphalt, and a pair of medics broke from their cover behind a line of armored trucks and angled cop cars. Connor recognized one of them—an older woman named Darcy who'd done more than her fair share of stitching his team up after a brutal raid. This time her attention was focused on the little boy he held close, her hands automatically reaching for Connor's charge.

As soon as she touched him, the boy screamed, a piercing cry sharp enough to cut past the racket of the raid. His fear punched into Connor's guts, flashing memories of the squalor Connor had found the boy in and the dead woman lying on the floor. Their shuffle to safety was a clumsy affair, dodging cop cars to reach the relative cover of the thicker-walled transports. Uniformed officers covered them, weapons trained on the ramshackle house.

"Shit, tell him to let go." The female paramedic swore. "Is he hurt?"

"I don't think so. Kid, she's here to take care of you," Connor said, moving forward to herd them all to cover. The other paramedic hustled beside them, trying to dislodge the boy from the other side. "I've got to get back in there. My team—"

"Morgan, we're clear," Yamamoto's voice echoed in Connor's headset. "Moving to the back of the house now. Team is all good. We've got this."

"And you're bleeding, Morgan," Darcy cut him off, holding her hand up so he could see the blood smeared over her palm. "Shut up and let me do my job. You die on me and I'll end up shoveling horse shit out of the cop stables for the rest of my life."

"Not going to die on you," he growled back. "Just probably a crease or something. Happens sometimes. Him first. Then we worry about me."

As soon as they got behind the SWAT vehicles, Connor was surrounded by people, some trying to dislodge the boy while Darcy attempted to undo his vest. She pushed at him to sit down on a lowered gurney and his world tilted slightly, his stomach grumbling at the vertigo hitting him square between the eyes. The boy's screams grew louder, more frantic, and Connor closed his arms over the child, rocking slightly despite the nerve-churning dizziness clawing at the back of his head.

"Hey, give him some time, okay," Connor ordered, cutting through everyone's chatter. He was beginning to feel the spots of pain along his back and arm as adrenaline bled out of his system. The blood on Darcy's hand hadn't been a lot, but something had gotten through somewhere, and he needed triage. "See if we can't get my vest off, and then we can work on getting him calmed down. He's scared. He just needs a little more time to feel safe before he can let go."

"He's going to have to let go of you at some point, Morgan," Darcy shot back. "Because no matter what he wants, you can't carry him forever. CPS is on their way, and then he'll be their problem."

CHAPTER TWO

SWIMMING THROUGH a sea of night-blue uniforms and polished metal stars was a clichéd horror Forest could have done without. A percussion roll of querulous voices hammered at him, wrapping him in a discordant storm. Somewhere behind him, Miki pushed them forward, the singer's hand firm on Forest's back. A break in the tight cluster turned out to be the edge of a nurses' station; then the world opened back up into a landscape of linoleum and bright white lights.

"Shit, what the hell is going on here?" Miki grumbled behind him. "Thought nothing bad happened."

"Not helping there, Sinjun." Forest gave one of the cops a tight smile, trying to place his face. "I've got to find out where Con is."

"Let me go ask somebody." Miki nodded his head toward one of the nurses sitting behind the counter a few feet away. "I tried calling Kane, but he didn't pick up. If she can't help me, then I'll try again."

"Connor's okay," Forest reminded himself. "Nothing serious or Kane would've told me."

And—the true sign of Connor's well-being—the ER wasn't full of Morgans.

"Hey, the nurse said he's down the hall." Miki appeared at Forest's elbow. "She said we can go in. He's in the fourth bay on the right."

"She didn't ask for any ID?" Fumbling at his pockets, Forest wasn't even sure he knew where his wallet was. "Suppose we were someone who wanted to hurt him? There's a lot of crazy people out there."

"Yeah, *you*." Miki shoved at Forest's shoulder, pushing them through the cluster of first responders standing in the middle of the walkway, talking about gunshot wounds and a raid they'd been on. "One, she recognized me and then recognized you. Two, even if any of the cops out here somehow let us pull some shit, what the fuck do you think Connor and Kane would do to somebody who came at them? Don't be stupid, and let's go find your husband."

A few yards in and a rumbling voice reached Forest's ears, its rakish velvet tones painted rich with a hint of Irish and stubborn authority. A man dressed in scrubs broke off from a small group of hospital workers, intending to cut them off, but Miki wouldn't be deterred. He angled Forest to the right, using the promise of Ireland and cop as his lighthouse among the chaos.

"Fuck off, dude," Miki warned off the medical tech. "He's going to go see his husband."

"You don't need to come down here, Mum," Kane said as he stepped out from behind a long beige curtain wrapped around an emergency room bed. Connor's younger brother stopped short when he spotted Miki and Forest headed his way. "Everything is going to be fine. Forest just got here, and Con's probably going to be released. I'll have him call you later."

When Forest saw Kane standing in front of them with his inspector's badge fixed to the leather gun harness he wore over a soft gray Henley, the reality of what had happened to his husband struck deep. Kane looked so much like Connor, it hurt. For a brief, wild moment, Forest cursed the universe, fear and terror screaming angrily inside of his soul that it should have been Kane lying there with bullet wounds and broken bones instead of Connor. Anyone but Connor.

Not his Connor.

The moment passed when reason filtered back into his brain, and the guilt in his heart must have been evident on his face because Miki—feral, gorgeous, and fierce Miki—muttered under his breath so only Forest could hear him.

"It's okay to be pissed off." Miki grabbed at the curtain, pulled it back, and stepped to the side so Forest could go past. "When shit like this happens to K, I want everybody else to bleed for it. So I get it. Let me go find out what's happening, and you go talk to the asshole who got shot."

"He's not an asshole," Forest protested. "Connor didn't ask for this."

"Sure he did. He's a Morgan," Miki snorted. "Gotta be something in Brigid's breast milk, because they all think they're fucking superheroes and bullets are just supposed to bounce off them."

"Hey, no talking about our mother and breast milk," Kane retorted. "That just makes this all weird."

"That's because there's something just not right about all of you," Miki shot back. "And what the fuck happened? Did everything go to shit?"

Behind the curtain, Forest's heart and life sat on a hospital bed, bandages fixed to his naked torso and a hospital blanket scrunched over Connor's lap. The gray sweatpants he wore to cover his long legs were probably Kane's—they carried a whiff of stale air and plastic from being buried in a gym bag—but the dark pink socks Con had on his feet were definitely hospital-issued, thin rubber stripes running over the soles to prevent slippage on the hospital's slick floors.

Connor's deep blue eyes were hooded and a little unfocused when his gaze swept over Forest. A rueful grin pulled at the left side of his mouth, bringing out the dimple Forest loved. The tightness in his expression was a clear sign he'd probably declined heavy pain medication, a Morgan family habit Forest could have happily beaten out of him.

That was one of the biggest problems of falling in love with a Morgan. They ran into burning buildings, tossed themselves into the raging waters, and scared the shit out of the people who loved them.

Seeing Connor's bare chest dappled with gauze and surgical tape didn't ease the anxiety and panic he'd stewed in his belly, its sourness burbling up as soon as he got that phone call from Kane.

That phone call.

Forest thought he'd been ready for it. He and Connor had talked about it. Even Brigid had given her take on how to handle the drowning emotions he could expect to flood him, but Forest realized nothing could have really prepared him for that solemn voice on the other end of the line telling him Con had been shot.

Stopping the band's practice hadn't even been a question. Guitars went down, and car keys were grabbed. The sharp, bitter razor cut of fear sliding along Forest's heart eased back when he was reassured Connor was okay, but it lingered, shadowing his thoughts. Marrying a Morgan meant the possibility of a sudden soul-breaking phone call, and even though they all knew the reality of the situation, it didn't make things any easier when a call came.

This time it was good news—or at least the best news that it could be, following a dangerous raid. Connor was okay—a bit banged up and sporting more than a few bruises but nothing he couldn't heal from. If only Forest could persuade his heart, so hard and so fast in his chest, then things would be okay. He knew what he was getting into when Con slid a wedding ring on his finger. Forest told himself time and time again that it didn't matter how long he had with Connor. So long as they were together, he would treasure every moment.

"I don't know if I want to hug you or puke all over you." Forest took in every inch of his husband he could see, noticing the smears of dried blood not quite wiped away from around his bandaged wounds. "If I puke, it's going to be nasty, because all I've had today is coffee and onion rings."

A step forward and his knees went out from under him. Forest would've fallen to the floor if Con hadn't grabbed at him, miles of tubing and wires connecting Connor to beeping machines stretched tight before Forest could regain his balance. His own hands were cold and unsteady as he stroked Connor's face, shaken deep with the fear he hadn't been able to bleed off. Connor smelled of blood and gunpowder, but the smile was still reassuring and full of love.

"I'll be taking the hug, if you don't mind," Connor teased. "But then we're going to have to put you in a chair, because they don't build these hospital beds big enough for the likes of my mother's children."

Their hug became a lifeline, a little treacherous from its angle but something Forest wouldn't have traded for the world. The rough scruff on Connor's jaw scraped at his neck, the press of his husband's lips on his too brief for his liking and, not for the first time, Forest wished Connor would grow his thick black hair long enough for Forest to hold on to.

"Are you sure you're okay?" Forest murmured, grateful for the strong thump of Connor's heartbeat resonating between them. "This really fucking scared me."

"That's why I asked Kane to give you a call. If the captain or chaplain called, I knew you'd be too worried." Connor's whisper tickled Forest's cheek. The hug grew tighter as Connor strengthening his hold on Forest's shoulders. "I was never not okay."

"Any time I get a phone call that starts off with *Connor's okay but*, I am always going to be scared." It was a light scold, but the fear crackling over his nerves still had a hold on Forest. "I'm just not ready to lose you."

"I'm not going anywhere, *a ghra*."

It was a promise Forest had heard before and one he knew Connor meant, but the universe had a sick sense of humor, and all it took was one small piece of metal and Forest's world would unravel.

Neither one of them wanted to let go, but a strained hiss from Connor was a red flag for Forest to step back. A hard-backed hospital chair was easy enough to drag over, but that would have meant letting go of Connor's hand. After a few tries to reach it with his foot, Forest gave in to the blighted reality of the matter and retrieved the chair.

"You brought Miki with you? Thought I heard him outside." Connor scratched at a strip of tape perilously close to his left nipple. At some point, for an unknown reason, someone had shaved spots away from the light dusting of soft black hair on Connor's muscular chest, adding bare skin dots to the plaid of white tape on his torso.

"No, Miki brought me," Forest replied. "He drove. I couldn't—I didn't trust myself. Damie and Rafe wanted to come, but I think if all of them showed up, it would be a zoo down here, and I didn't want to deal with that."

"So your solution was Miki?" Connor pressed, catching up Forest's trembling fingers in his firm grasp. "That is not a life choice I would've made. He barely passed his driving test, remember?"

"Says the guy who goes through locked doors with people shooting at him on the other side of them."

"Okay, fair point, love," Connor said ruefully. "I'm just glad you got here in one piece instead of ending up in the bed next to me."

"He isn't that bad of a driver," he defended the band's singer. "It helped that he was pissed off you got shot. Said it gave him focus."

"Both of you knew it wasn't serious, right? A piece of the bullet got in between things and just tore the top off my skin a bit." Connor rubbed at Forest's palm. "I took more damage falling. They think I might've fractured something other than my ribs. I might be in an ortho boot for a few weeks if I fractured something in my foot. If that happens, then I'm riding a desk for a while."

"Would that be so bad?" He ran his thumb over Connor's firm jaw. "Yeah, I don't know what I'm thinking. You'd be chewing everybody's head off in about a week."

Connor was too larger-than-life to look this vulnerable, but the pain in his face nipped at the edges of his bravado, and Forest edged closer to the bed. The heat coming off Connor's body was a reassurance

Forest hadn't known he needed. A small bruise marred Connor's rugged features, a spread of purple and blue along his right cheekbone. Despite being a large, muscular presence on an almost-too-small hospital gurney, Connor looked slightly torn apart and raw.

The sight of Connor hurting dug into Forest's guts. He knew better. He'd known what he was signing up for when he first fell in love with the no-holds-barred SWAT officer who'd pushed his way into Forest's life. Connor was there for the most heart-wrenching moment, when he lost Frank, and celebrated every good thing that had happened between them since then. Connor not only offered Forest his love but also his family, a warm chaotic mess of an Irish clan who immediately took him in and loved him.

Outside of the enclosed area, the hospital sounded like a battlefield, shouts for medical personnel and occasionally the angry cries of someone proclaiming his innocence. Someone wearing a SFPD uniform peeked in past the curtain for a brief moment—too quick for Forest to see their face—then moved on, hunting a different quarry than the SWAT officer who'd taken a few hits.

"So what happened?" Forest rubbed at his face, the relief of finally seeing Connor leaving him fatigued and oddly anxious. He must've cried on the way over, or at least it felt like it. "What went wrong? I thought you guys weren't the lead team going in. Isn't that how that works?"

"Yeah, most of the time." Connor's expression shifted, a flash of anger and sorrow muddying his blue gaze. "It was just a tough ride this time. There was this little kid there. Dirty face, big eyes, and right next to a dead woman. Things were going bad at the back of the house, and it was moving up to the front."

"So you grabbed him and ran?"

"Yeah. I grabbed him and ran." He shrugged, wincing as he lowered his shoulder back down. "They're checking him out down the hall, I think. Tell you the truth, he reminded me a lot of Miki."

"Did he bite you?" Forest chuckled when Connor shot him a grin. "Tell me that's something Miki wouldn't do."

"That or punch the shit out of you. But no, it was more his face. Something in his eyes," his husband drawled. "I don't know how to explain it, but it was like I was picking up something wild and hurt. I felt like I could have lost a finger or maybe even my hand, but I had to get him out of there. The kid let me grab him and just held on tight. He trusted me to keep him safe. Didn't say a thing. Just… held on."

"But he's okay?"

"I don't know," Connor confessed. "CPS has him. And for some stupid reason, I just can't shake the bad feeling I've got over that. I know I should trust the system. And I know things are different compared to how it was when you and Miki were in it, but I also know everybody is stretched thin. Best we can hope for is that they find someone in his family to take care of him."

"Do you think the dead woman was his mother?" The conversation was bringing up memories Forest would rather have left in the shadows of his mind. As far as he'd come—as lucky as he had been with Frank taking him in—there were still weeping wounds buried inside of him. "I guess that's the only place to start to look."

"I've pulled a lot of kids out of places like that before," Connor replied. "For some reason, this one is just hitting me hard. I don't know why."

"How about if we work on getting you home so you can heal up?" Forest rose and kissed Connor on the mouth. His husband tasted of smoke and sweat, but the warmth of his lips soothed away the last of Forest's anxiety. "Let me go see if I can find someone to cut you loose, and more importantly, what do we have to do to get you into a shower? Because you really stink."

"Even worse than the guys when you were doing that road trip tour in the van?" he teased.

"Yeah, worse than that." Wrinkling his nose, Forest sniffed at his husband again. "Okay, maybe Rafe after he had that brussels-sprouts-and-refried-bean tostada has you beat. But not by much."

IF HE closed his eyes, Connor could almost see them transported back in time, blood brothers sworn to stick together through thick and thin. And they had, even as life and tragedies tried to tug them apart. He and the other three tightened their bond, weathering everything from Rafe's addiction to Connor's unexpected love for Forest. Huddled together on the widow's walk of the Morgans' family home, he, Kane, their cousin Sionn, and their adopted brother, Rafe, sat protected from the light drizzle by a jut of the roof, their bellies warmed by a small bottle of whiskey Sionn brought with him.

Night hadn't completely fallen, but it was threatening the horizon, sipping away at the gray glare of the bleached-out cloudy sky. The sounds of the Morgan clan playing some kind of game bounced up from the main floor below, the french doors thrown open to let the cool air flow through the house. He heard Forest's laughter bursting out after something unseen happened, a rolling burnished silver sound Connor held close to his heart.

It amazed him he could pick out his husband's laughter amid all the noise. Even calling Forest his husband humbled him. Connor never expected to fall in love with another man. That was never something he'd even contemplated much less acted on, but after he saw Forest—got to know him—he couldn't shake the man out of his heart, and he hadn't even really tried. But it was hard to swallow the shift his life would have to take. Connor had a life plan he'd been following since he was young. He would wear an SFPD star, like his father. He would marry a fierce woman, someone who would be his partner until death tore them apart, and hopefully—with a lot of luck—he would raise his children up to be good people.

Forest definitely threw him for a loop.

And now he was faced with another unshakable grip on his soul.

He couldn't shake off the responsibility he felt toward the little boy from the raid, and he didn't know how to get rid of the haunting memory of the boy's heartbreaking gaze when they took him from Connor's arms.

"How long do you have to wear that thing?" Rafe asked, holding the whiskey bottle out for Connor to take. "Looks uncomfortable as shit."

"Four weeks," he responded, grateful for his friend's warmth next to him. The chill in the air would have been fine if he had worn thicker sweatpants, but they'd been in a hurry to get to the family's weekly gathering, so he'd thrown on the first thing he saw, a pair of thin cotton joggers. Their legs were wide enough to go over his boots but offered little protection from the occasional biting wind whistling over San Francisco's hills.

"Better than a cast," Sionn interjected. "When I screwed up my knee and they put all that plaster over me, I wanted to saw it off after five days. How are you going to work out with that thing? Can't see you sitting on the sidelines for a month without wanting some gym time."

"I didn't even think about that," Kane said, taking the bottle after Connor took a burning sip of whiskey. "Leg days are definitely out, and how are you going to anchor if you can't put pressure on that foot?"

"There is something seriously wrong with the three of you if working out is what you're focused on." Rafe shook his head. "If I were you, I'd be more worried about how you're going to have sex."

"Trust Andrade to go right to the crotch." Sionn chuckled. "Not everything is about sex, Rafe."

"It is if you're doing your life right," he shot back, then yelped when Kane leaned over and punched him on the shoulder. "What the fuck, K?"

"Keep in mind that you're sleeping with our brother," Kane playfully cautioned. "The last thing I want to hear about is you and Quinn having sex."

"That's a shame," Rafe sneered back. "You might learn a few things—"

"I don't have any problems with sex and Forest." Connor cut through the badgering before things got heated. Even playful banter sometimes got hot, and while there wouldn't be a fight, things did get a little bit dirty. "I've got a physical therapist who's helping me out. If my foot's wrapped up the right way, I can do water therapy to keep my legs up. He thinks I'm okay to do everything else, but not to overdo it."

"That's good," Kane murmured. "Don't want you to end up with chicken legs. You'd look stupider than you already do."

"So they have you doing desk work?" Sionn chimed in, steering the conversation in another direction. "How's that going? Must be driving you nuts, not being able to do the job."

"I'm doing everything except knocking through the doors," Connor said. "But it does give me a lot of time to think, and just between us, that kid I took out of that raid?"

"The raid that put you into this thing?" Kane gestured toward the orthopedic boot on Connor's foot. "And got you shot?"

"Yeah, that one." He gratefully took the bottle back when Sionn passed it over, then took a moment to savor the burn of the whiskey in his throat. "I can't get the kid out of my brain, and I'm wondering—not that I've done anything—but I'm wondering if Forest and I can take him in."

"Like to raise?" Rafe let out a low whistle. "Fuck, Con. You sure you weren't hit on the head?"

"Yeah, I'm sure," Connor replied, picking at the bottle's label with his thumbnail. "I just want to know if he's okay. Or if he even has family. But if he doesn't, we all know what's out there for him, and I just can't let that happen. I just can't let the thought of that go."

"Have you talked to Forest about it?" Kane slipped the bottle out of Connor's hands.

"No," he admitted softly. "You guys are the first I'm talking to about it."

"Well, big brother," Kane *tsk*ed, "I'm not the one to be handing out marriage advice, but Forest should be the one you talk to about this. Maybe tonight instead of trying to figure out how to do something out of the *Kama Sutra* while wearing that boot, you bring up the kid instead."

CHAPTER THREE

THE AROMATIC punch of brewing coffee greeted Connor as he came in through the back door. The morning chill followed him, a hint of rain threaded through the wind. The cold breeze bit down on the damp spots on his shirt where he hadn't quite dried off enough from his shower at the gym, and he quickly shut the door behind him, shivering slightly in the kitchen's warmth.

He'd spent countless hours renovating the old Victorian he'd purchased at a foreclosure sale, a tired old woman of a house beaten down by time and neglect. He'd restored every inch of wood paneling and vintage finishings to bring the house back to its former beauty, but the kitchen was where he'd gone rogue, tearing down the walls between the old dark space and an enclosed side porch. Sash windows running along one wall let in the outside light, brightening the kitchen even on a dreary gray day. The majority of the large appliances were skillfully hidden behind the faux cabinet fronts, and the enormous center island gave him enough space to prep the prodigious amount of food it took to feed his family. But more importantly, there was more than enough space to put an old art deco dresser against the wall where the coffee machine—unquestionably the hardest working piece of equipment in the house—burbled away, slowly filling its glass pot.

As enticing as the coffee was, Connor was drawn more to the lanky seductive man bobbing his head to whatever music was flowing through his wireless headphones.

The worn pair of jeans slung low over Forest's hips had probably been plucked from a thrift-store shelf years before Connor ever met the drummer. And he had no idea who the band was on his husband's faded black T-shirt, but judging from the cities listed on the back, they'd hit every small town along the Eastern Seaboard. Forest's dirty-blond hair was pulled back into a low ponytail, but several strands had escaped, feathering down over his sharp cheekbones. Standing at the sink, one of his bare feet tapping in time with the music, he scrubbed at one of the casserole dishes they'd taken to the Morgans' weekly family gathering, optimistically soaked overnight in the hopes of loosening some baked-on cheese. The slight pout of Forest's lower lip and the rigid set of his muscular shoulders told Connor the soaking hadn't been successful.

Leaning against the threshold, Connor took a moment to drink in the sight of the man he'd fallen in love with. Shaped by years of drumming and moving heavy sound equipment, Forest's lean, sculpted body still struck Connor with a curious, hungry longing. The musician wasn't anything like Connor had expected his spouse to be. He'd always thought he would fall for a woman more like his mother—a fierce and protective personality willing to go a few rounds with whoever got in her way. Instead, he'd fallen into a pair of doe-brown eyes filled with tragedy and old pain and the sweet, vulnerable soul living behind them.

And Connor never regretted asking Forest to be a part of his life. Now he just had to convince his husband to take a risk neither one of them ever imagined they would face.

"Hey," Connor called out from where he stood. "I'm—"

"What the fuck?" Forest's hand came up out of the soapy water, clenched around a dripping spatula. His startled expression turned sheepish when he realized it was Connor, and he pushed aside his headphones with his forearm. Dropping the utensil back into the sink, he shook his head, then resumed scrubbing. "Don't do that. Scared the crap out of me."

"Sorry," he said, stopping for a second to kiss Forest's nape. "But you have to admit, love, if you have those things on, your mind is elsewhere."

"Yeah, whatever." Forest rinsed the soap off the casserole dish and set it on the drainer. "Coffee should almost be done. Did you eat? I can make you something."

"I think just coffee." Con made his way over to the sputtering machine. "How about if I get us each a cup and we go sit down in the living room? I got something I want to talk about."

"You're divorcing me and taking up with Mrs. Bernstein?" Forest teased, drying his hands on a dish towel. "Sure, she's eighty-five years old, but she makes a mean brown-butter chocolate-chip cookie."

"Don't tempt me," he *tsk*ed back. "Stronger men have fallen for her baking artistry."

"Well, then, lucky for me she just dropped some off. I don't know what's with people like you who have to get up at six in the morning to go to the gym or power walk five miles, but you should probably see somebody about it." Forest grabbed a plastic container off the kitchen counter. "Can you carry both of the cups without spilling, or do you need some help, Igor?"

"You are so lucky I love you," Connor grumbled back. "And probably extra lucky because you've got the cookies. Go on. I'm right behind you."

FOREST WAS settled on the couch when Connor joined him. He looked incredibly young, legs pulled up with his feet tucked under him and nestled back into a pile of pillows. The container of cookies lay open on the coffee table, a tempting tickle of chocolate and butter mingling with the aroma of coffee and cream. Forest took the cup Connor held out to him, drew it in for a sniff, then took a tentative sip.

"It's been almost a year since I accidentally added in that salt," Connor protested. "And that never would've happened if it hadn't been so close to the coffee machine."

"You salt someone's coffee, they are never going to trust you again," his husband replied with a smirk. "Have a cookie. And let me guess, you want to talk about whatever sent you and the other three up to the widow's walk yesterday, right?"

"Yeah," he admitted, carefully sitting down on the other side of the couch and angling his booted foot to rest it on the support bar of the coffee table. "I needed to get a reality check on something."

Forest took a sip, then asked, "What did they say?"

"Well," Connor responded, saluting Forest with his coffee cup. "They told me I needed to check with my reality."

"So what did you want to talk about?"

Connor could read Forest's mood shift. Anxiety threaded through his even temperament, threatening to eat away at the musician's good nature. He set his cup down on the coffee table, then reached over to rub at his husband's knee, hoping his touch would ease some of Forest's tension. Forest, like Miki, grew up in a world of uncertainties and broken promises, leaving him uneasy about any type of stability and happiness. Every serious moment, every need to talk, was a potential abandonment on the horizon, no matter how many times Connor reassured Forest he was loved and going nowhere.

If anything, the fragile vulnerability in Forest's expression was a mirror of the face of the boy he'd found in the drug house, and his heart ached to see it in his husband's eyes.

"It's nothing bad," Connor promised in a soft whisper. "If anything, I think it's a chance for us to change someone's life for the good, but I know that we need to talk it out, and it's not going to be easy."

"Okay, what are you talking about?" Forest let Connor take his mug out of his hands to set it down on the table. Despite the hot coffee, Forest's fingers were chilled. "You sound way too serious, even for you."

"The first thing I want to tell you is that—other than asking the guys what they thought about me talking to you about it—I haven't really even looked into it. I didn't want it to go that far without seeing how you felt." Taking Forest's hands in his, he continued, "Remember I talked about the little boy I pulled out?"

"Yeah, you got that thing on your foot because of it," Forest pointed out. "What about him? Did something happen to him? Is he okay?"

"I don't know," Connor admitted. By habit, he began tracing the calluses on Forest's fingers, a familiar path they often took when they spoke about uncomfortable things. "That's what I want to talk to you about. I want to see if they will let us foster him—if he's even able to be fostered—because I can't stop thinking about the kind of shit he's seen and everything that he's going to have to face in the system. So what I'm asking you is, what do you think about me—about us—bringing him home?"

LOST IN the pounding rhythm of his conflicting emotions, Forest didn't hear the studio door open. His mind took him through countless songs, every percussive beat hammering away at the odd anger mixed in with fear filling him. He'd started off with the blues, its sliding trills quickly giving way to heavier sounds, darker threads of bass notes and snares. It wasn't until a shadow fell across his tom-tom that he realized he wasn't alone.

"Fucking hell." His heart was in his throat, and Forest exhaled hard, seeing Miki standing in front of him, holding a stack of what looked like peanut butter and jelly sandwiches on a plate. "That's twice today somebody scared the crap out of me."

"You've been here a couple of hours, so I figured by now, you might be hungry." The lean singer held the plate a little higher. "I poked my head in when I came home from my walk with Dude and saw your car, but it didn't sound like you wanted some company."

If there was one good thing about joining Crossroads Gin, it was the deepening friendship he'd formed with Miki St. John. As intimidating as Miki was as a musician, he was even scarier personally. A little bit younger than Forest and raised on the streets, he'd endured unimaginable pain and horror, sharpening the fangs of his personality. But buried under the antisocial aloofness beat the heart of a dedicated friend and someone who loved deeply and unconditionally. Once taken into Miki's intimate circle, a person was never left in doubt of his loyalty and commitment to them. Even though they had shared experiences, Forest knew he'd had a much easier time in life than Miki, and while they had a family in the Morgans, Miki counted Forest as a brother, a connection he cherished.

The blond terrier trotting in behind Miki longingly eyed the plate of sandwiches and kept his attention on the stack while Miki settled down on one of the love seats at the back of his at-home music studio. The massive warehouse Miki purchased during the height of his first band's success had been converted into a comfortable home. He had turned all of the docking bays into garages, with the exception of the one closest to the main street. That bay and the warehouse space behind it was a fully working studio and storage for the musical instruments Miki and his brother-in-all-but-blood, Damien, acquired along the way.

It was a comfortable space filled with soft furniture and a separate area for sound mixing and recording, but mostly, it served as a spot all of the band members could go to when they needed some space from life. Bright and soundproofed, it bore the brunt of their arguments and elation, as well as the time they needed to be alone, losing themselves in the music they created. Still, Forest was grateful to see Miki, even as his arms and shoulders ached from the nonstop drumming he'd done since he arrived.

"I think I need a shower." Forest didn't have to look to know he was soaked through with sweat. "Let me grab one quick, if you don't mind."

"That's why they built a full bathroom," Miki said, using his toe to discourage Dude from sniffing at the sandwich plate he'd balanced on the back of the couch. "Hurry up, though. You'd think this asshole here hadn't been fed breakfast."

After scrubbing himself down quickly, Forest dug through the pile of clean clothes they'd all left behind at one time or another. Feeling better in a clean pair of sweatpants and someone's old T-shirt, he rejoined Miki in the studio and gave his friend a grin when he spotted Dude polishing off a jam-speckled crust.

"Did he help himself, or did you give him one?" He sat down on the battered wing chair they'd dragged in from a Tenderloin thrift shop, its once vibrant paisley upholstery now faded from time and constant use. Still, it was comfortable and nearly wide enough to be another love seat, with plenty of room for Forest to sit cross-legged.

"I gave him one," Miki admitted, holding the plate out to Forest. A collection of ice-cold water bottles sat on a milk crate between them, and Forest grabbed one, along with a sandwich. "It works out. He likes the end bits."

In true Miki fashion, he said nothing to Forest about coming into the studio to work out his aggressions or ask about what was bothering him. Instead, the singer sat in silence with the occasional comment to the blond terrier lying belly up at Miki's feet, groaning in pleasure when Miki used his bare toes to scratch the dog's stomach.

They ate in silence for a few minutes after Forest surreptitiously examined the peanut butter and jelly sandwich. Miki had odd ideas of what went together for food. Sometimes they worked out, like the jalapeño jelly and cream cheese on a waffle, but there had been the occasional what-the-hell combination that gave even Forest, who wasn't a picky eater, a bit of trouble. The bowl of mayonnaise and canned peas still haunted Forest's nightmares, despite having seen the singer eat it quite a few times during their friendship. The sandwich appeared safe, but he couldn't identify the jelly, other than it was pink but didn't seem to have any actual fruit in it.

A few bites in, Forest still had no clue, but it didn't taste like fish or anything weird, so he kept eating.

"Guava," Miki said through a mouthful of food. "I saw you looking."

"Not judging," Forest responded, chewing carefully.

Miki side-eyed him. "Bullshit. Not like I'm feeding you sardines and rice again."

"That didn't taste bad," he protested. "I just wasn't expecting it to be so spicy. I thought all of the red was tomato sauce. It was still good."

"Huh." No one could do noncommittal scoffing like the band's singer, and Miki's shrug only added to the light admonishment of Forest's examination of the food.

After another minute, Forest glanced over at Miki. "Did Kane tell you what they all talked about when they disappeared up to their clubhouse?"

Mike leaned forward to give the dog a bit of bread and looked up through the dark hair that had fallen over his face, his hazel green eyes studying Forest for a moment. Then he responded, "I can barely keep track of my own shit. I don't get into anyone else's unless they ask me to. Kane usually doesn't talk about what goes on between the Four Musketeers, and I don't usually tell him what we talk about with the band."

"I kinda need someone to bounce some shit off," he admitted, trying to find any thread of his conflicting emotions to grab on to so he could begin to process what Connor proposed. "I don't know what to do or even what to think. My mind right now is really screwed up, and I don't think I can talk it out with Con."

"What happened?" Miki leaned back, moving slightly to give the terrier room to join him on the couch. "You guys okay?"

"I think so. Hell, now I don't know." Panic flared in his belly, a kernel of doubt planted there from years of neglect and uncertainty. "You know he's always talked about having kids. That's really important to him."

"Well, if any of us ever have kids, you two are the best ones for it," Miki pointed out. "Does he want one *now*? I mean, those kind of take time to grow."

"He wants to foster the kid he rescued from his last raid. The one he carried out." Forest put the remains of his sandwich down on the plate, his appetite soured by the rumbling in his stomach. "Maybe even adopting."

Miki sat in contemplative silence, then asked, "I thought you guys were going to do the surrogate thing, with you and Kiki making a baby soup. He doesn't want to do that anymore? I'm kind of lost here."

"That was the plan," Forest said. "But now here's this little boy, and there's just a lot to unpack there. I think I'm going to say a lot of shitty things right now because I don't know how else to say them."

Miki shrugged. "Sometimes it's the only way to get it out. Go ahead."

Sighing heavily, Forest tapped at his knees, letting the rhythm grab at his thoughts. "This isn't a for-sure thing, because he wanted to talk to me before he even asked about the kid. I mean, it's the right thing to do, but now I have all of these questions I don't have any answers to."

"Like what?"

"I realized as Connor was talking that I've never actually been around any kids before," he murmured, staring at his drum kit, finally finding someplace to start examining how he felt. "I mean, he has, but shit, I don't even know what it's like to *be* a kid. I kind of realized driving over here. That kind of fucked me up because there's this little boy who's starting off like you and I did but I can change that—Connor and I change that—but I don't know if I can. I don't know what the fuck to do. I thought we were going to have a kid from scratch and even that scares the hell out of me. Suppose I screw him up worse? Suppose he needs fixing and I can't do it?"

"He's probably already going to be screwed up," Miki interjected. "I mean, it's a given considering where he was found. How old is he?"

"Don't know," Forest replied. "Connor hasn't talked to anyone, remember?"

"Yeah, so you're kind of starting out the whole thing with absolutely no answers." Miki bit his lower lip and cocked his head. "You don't even know if you guys can foster him, but you definitely have to figure stuff out."

"I'm also kind of worried about—and this is going to sound stupid, maybe—but Connor says he thinks the kid is mixed. Maybe Asian or Hispanic and European. The race thing isn't the issue. I just… there's this whole thing about…." Forest struggled to nail down what he was trying to say. "If we take him in, how do we make sure he has a connection to his culture? I can't be—"

"White saviors?" Miki drawled. "I mean, it's a thing. Do you think that's where you're coming from? That you guys are somehow going to save him from who he's from instead of the shit he was born into?"

"I don't know," he admitted. "I look at you and you're half Thai—"

"So they tell me," the singer teased.

"See, that's kind of what I'm talking about." Forest exhaled sharply. "I know you're exploring that a little bit, but do you think you'll ever feel connected to your mom's culture?"

"No matter what I do, dude, I'm always going to be a tourist there," Miki replied softly, his fingers ruffling his dog's fur. "I don't know if anyone can make the connection to any culture unless they're steeped in it. Not going to lie and tell you I don't get pissed off about it. I get angry about a lot of things. I'm never going to know her. I know *about* her. I know she loved me, but it's all just words.

"Whether or not you and Connor take this kid in—if you *can* take this kid in—he's already started life in the red," the singer pointed out. "He's in the system, and he's going to be moved around. In a perfect world, they'd match him up with some people who could teach him where he came from, but you and I both know that's not going to happen. They're going to try to make sure he gets fed and has some place to sleep. Maybe go to school. I don't know. He could also have a family that they've found and he's already got a home with them. We don't know any of it. You're scared about fucking up some kid that is already fucked up."

"I just feel like I'm a bad person for even being scared about it," Forest whispered. "But even if we did the IVF thing, I could screw that kid up too. I don't know what I'm doing, and now I'm wondering if I should even have kids."

"Truthfully, I think it's good you've got questions, because you're not bullshitting yourself." Miki took a sip of water, swallowed slowly, then said, "I think you'd be good for any kid—recycled or from scratch—because you *care*. You're not making it some kind of fairy tale where everyone is wearing matching outfits on Sunday and Thursday is when you have meatloaf for dinner. I don't have any answers for you, dude. Shit, nobody has answers for you. Are you going to fuck up? Yeah, you are. Everybody does. But I also tell you, if you guys do take this kid in, he'll be lucky to have you. Because if you are half as good of a dad as you are a friend, then the kid will be okay. *That* much I know."

CHAPTER FOUR

FOREST FOUND his husband in the sunroom at the back of their Victorian home. The broad chairs were chosen to be comfortable for a Morgan's too-large frame, and despite the dampness in the air, the space was warm and cozy, heated by a small wood stove Connor had refurbished after finding it at an estate sale. Big fuzzy rugs provided insulation from the cool tile floors and were easily rolled up on hot summer days. A half-empty coffee cup kept Connor company, his attention buried in a book and his injured foot resting on an ottoman, the ortho boot discarded and lying on the floor.

"Hey," Forest called out softly, nodding at Connor's cup when his husband looked up. "Do you want a refill?"

"I don't know," Connor replied, the Irish thick in his words. There was a lot of emotion in his tone, but Forest couldn't separate out the threads of it amid his own trepidation. A sweet smile softened the mood, and then Connor sighed. "Are you okay? Are *we* okay?"

"Yeah, I just had to work out some things in my head, and I didn't know where to start." Forest closed the distance between them, then picked up Connor's cup to take it into the kitchen with him. "I went down to the studio to just let my brain go where it wanted to go. Kept going until my arms hurt, took a shower because I smelled, dug through clothes we left down there to find something to wear, then had a peanut butter and guava jelly sandwich with Miki."

"I was wondering about the sweatpants. They look a little big on you, and I don't think I've ever seen you in orange." Connor put his finger between the open pages of his book, closed it partially but kept his place. "Are you looking to talk, or do you need more time?"

Forest stared at the man he had sworn to love beyond death. Their journey hadn't been an easy one, and there were still a lot of times when he wondered if Connor had made a mistake and would one day wake up to discover he'd married someone totally ill-suited to him. He was almost too scared to think about *any* future they would have, almost living each day as it came because looking ahead was too frightening, too much like accepting he deserved happiness. Bringing a child into their home— even simply fostering one—was a monumental step forward toward that uncertain future. But the ruggedly handsome Irish cop he'd fallen in love with deserved more than existing in a limbo of Forest's anxiety.

"I want to talk it out," he said, giving Connor a slight salute with the cold brew. "Let me change into something less eye bleeding, and I'll come out here with some hot coffee for us. Okay?"

"Okay." Connor snagged Forest's free hand, then lifted it toward him, kissing the inside of Forest's wrist. "Just remember, I love you above all others, and anything we do, we do together. I want you to know that, *a ghra*."

"It's hard to trust that." Sending Connor an apologetic smile, Forest squeezed his husband's hand, then let go. "And it's not that I don't trust you. I don't trust *me*. Or at least I don't trust life, because it was shitty for so long and now things are good, so I keep waiting for something bad to happen."

Connor snorted, opening his book. "And here I thought being Catholic wasn't contagious."

THEY ENDED up sharing a couch in the living room, the arrival of the cold rain driving them indoors. Wedged into a corner, Connor sat with his booted foot up on the cushions, waiting for Forest to get comfortable on the other side. Cradling a hot cup of coffee in one hand and brushing Forest's outstretched leg with the other, he recognized his husband's discomfort, especially when Forest cradled a throw pillow against his stomach. There were still places inside of Forest's soul Connor couldn't reach—dark hurtful spots bruising the drummer's good nature. He hated their existence, the whispering little voices telling Forest he wasn't good enough.

Still, Connor could count on Forest to talk to him, to be willing to open up and be vulnerable, something Connor himself struggled with.

"I have a lot of questions," Forest started. "And I know you probably don't have all of the answers because you haven't talked to anybody about him—the boy—so I promise not to get frustrated if you don't know."

"Fair enough," he replied. "I didn't want to talk to anybody about the possibility of fostering him or anything until I spoke to you. It was kind of six of one and half a dozen of another. I didn't know if you would be angry that I reached out without talking to you first or if it would be worse if I didn't have any answers. Like I said, I don't even know if we can take him in or if they've found family for him."

"No, I get that." After picking up his own steaming cup, Forest cradled it in front of the scrunched up pillow and stared down into its milky depths. "We don't even know his name, right?"

"I never heard one," Connor admitted. "But I think we're getting ahead of ourselves. And just so you don't think you're alone in this, I am scared shitless about doing this. I don't know if we *can* do this or if we're the right people for him. How about if we start off with something you're worried about and then I add to it."

"Shit, I've got so many issues." Forest finally took a sip of his coffee, huffing out a breath after he swallowed. "You said he's mixed, or at least you thought he is. You're as Irish as green soap, and I'm white street trash. I'm not worried about anyone giving a shit because he's a different ethnicity. I'm worried that were not going to do right by him with knowing where he comes from or at least knowing the culture he's from."

"That's valid. We both have very different experiences in the world from him, and I don't know what difficulties he might face, but it's something we're going to have to watch out for, I guess." He traced a circle around Forest's ankle bone, thinking about what his husband said. "To be honest, that's not something I thought about. I think I was just focused on giving him a better life than what I think he will have in the system."

"I just want to make sure that we aren't looking at this like we're rescuing him from himself. And I don't know if that makes sense because it's a jumble in my head, but I think it's something we really need to care about." Sighing, Forest looked up at Connor. "I'm not trying to make it seem like we're charging in on our white horses to save him. I don't have any cultural connection to anything. Even with Frank, Thanksgiving and Christmas were pretty much hot dogs from a convenience store and a cold beer. You're the one with a cultural identity, with actual family traditions, but I guess I just don't want him to lose who he is."

"The Morgans do have a tendency to try to fix things." He pursed his mouth, then ruefully smiled. "And people. My mother comes to mind."

"She's been better about it," Forest pointed out. "But that's probably something else we need to be mindful of. You guys are pretty overwhelming. Everyone coming into it reacts differently."

"Look at Quinn," Connor said. "He was born a Morgan and still has issues. Or rather Mum has issues. It wasn't easy for either one of them. There wasn't the kind of support there is now for people like Quinn and my mom. That's actually something I was worried about with the kid. He's going to have issues that neither one of us will understand, and we're going to have to be willing to get help when things come up."

"Yeah, we are." Nodding, Forest relaxed a bit, resting his back on the couch arm. "I think we also have to talk about what our schedule is going to look like and how we're going to deal with things when you're working and I go out on the road."

The reality Forest described struck Connor hard. He'd gotten used to his husband being home, or at least within a phone call's reach. As much as music shaped Forest's life, the working piece of it barely touched them. The one road trip the band had taken was a short one, a cross-country, small-dive affair they went on to solidify their relationship. The idea of Forest playing in larger venues and stadium arenas for months on end was something he hadn't contemplated.

"You didn't think about that, did you?" Forest probed gently. "And I'm not trying to pick a fight, but did you forget I'm in a band and what that means? Or at least what that means to me?"

Connor paused for a moment, thinking about how to answer. Forest's gaze grew wary. He was bracing himself for what Connor was going to say, but for the life of him, anything Connor came up with wasn't going to go well.

Taking a deep breath, he went with the simple truth, trusting the bond between them. "You're right. I didn't think about it. I didn't think about what it would mean to our lives, even before I brought up fostering. I guess in my mind, Crossroads Gin is a group of guys you play with and not... I know it's real. I know it's important to you but—"

"It's not a hobby, Con," Forest cut through Connor's words with a slightly sharp tone. "Sorry, I told you I wasn't trying to pick a fight, and it's not fair for me to be pissed off because you answered honestly.

I'm guessing in your head The Sound and the coffee shop are my main businesses, but that's not how I make my living. Even before the band, I was a studio drummer. Damie asking me to be a part of Crossroads was huge. It gives me a chance to share what I do—write my own parts to a song—instead of playing other people's music. Even if we just played dive bars for the rest of our lives, being a part of a band is something I've always dreamed of. I don't want to give it up."

"No." Connor shook his head. "I know that. I just didn't really grasp the enormity of it. It's not like I didn't know Rafe when he played with his other band, and I listened to Sinner's Gin so… I guess I don't think of you guys being rock stars. I just can't see you in private planes and demanding all of the yellow M&Ms be taken out of the candy jars backstage."

"I don't think we're rock stars," Forest snorted. "Damie might think he is, and Rafe's already played at doing that, so this time around he's got his head on better, but rock star is a stretch. I played for years, drumming in a closed box for other people. Now it's my stuff, my bass line. I don't know where it's going to go, but for the first time in my life, I am a part of something that I didn't know I really wanted. Or maybe I just didn't let myself dream about. And I feel shitty because I'm being selfish about it."

"You're not being selfish," he reassured his husband. "If anything, I did you dirty by not understanding what being a part of the band meant to you. Or even what being in the band is. That's on me, *a ghra*."

"You're a part of SWAT. That's not a nine-to-five job, Connor." Forest jerked his foot when Connor's fingers touched his heel, a forgotten ticklish spot Connor usually avoided. "We don't know how old he is or if he's in school. Or if he's ever been in school. If we take him in, then we're going to have to have some kind of schedule, because kids come with a lot of stuff and activities. And if he needs therapy, we have to work really hard to make sure that happens."

"I am not going to say we won't get help," he replied. "I don't know what help is going to look like, but it could be my family, or maybe we even hire someone to help out with things. That's something we're going to have to figure out once we know what the situation is. But for right now, there are just too many unknowns."

"I think the first thing that we need to decide on is if we're really going to do it." Forest reached over and set his coffee cup down on the table, his arm still clutched around the pillow against his torso. "I'm scared. I'm scared of screwing up a kid because I don't know what I'm doing. But I'm also scared that he's going to need more than what we can give him and neither one of us will want to admit that because we don't want to fail him. I don't even know how to tell something is working, or what happens when CPS comes in and we think we're doing okay but they take him away from us? What about then?"

"I don't know, love." Connor set aside his cup, then inched as close to Forest as he could, mindful of the awkward device on his injured foot. "We're borrowing trouble right now with all of that. The question we can answer is are we going to see if it's possible to bring him here, to bring him home? And if you can't say yes, that's okay."

Forest let himself be pulled in, turning around carefully so he could lean his back against Connor's chest. "Doing this probably hurts your ribs."

"Not doing this will hurt my heart." He chuckled when Forest snorted at him. "How about if I reach out to somebody in social services and see what the situation is? We don't have to make any decisions."

"I know that this is important to you. And if someone came to me when I was a little kid and said hey, you can come live in this house and get fed and go to school, I would've gone." Forest shrugged, then leaned his head back against Connor's shoulder. "I mean, that's kind of what happened with Frank. I can't promise you I'll be good at this, helping raise a kid. But if I sit and think about it, my gut tells me this is something we should at least try. You already asked him to trust you once, and he did. He knows you'll carry him. Just like I know you'll carry me. So yeah, go talk to those people, and let's see what we have to do to bring him home."

"MS. STICE?" Connor knocked on the partially open door, hoping he'd found the right office. The directions he'd gotten were a bit fuzzy, spurts of information from an intake officer holding a phone conversation with someone about the lack of air conditioning in the main hall and an assistant herding a bunch of teenagers through the building while looking for a volunteer coordinator.

Dressed in his daily gear and uniform, his appearance at the counter drew alarmed looks, and he tried not to notice the suspicious whispers between two of the taller teen boys at the back of the group. A smile at the assistant seemed to only make her more nervous, and she quickly shuffled her charges past him. Securing a room number and a general way toward one of the halls branching off the main reception area, Connor left the chaos behind him and plunged deeper into the labyrinth of mingled departments and chopped-up office spaces.

Like most government departments, Child Protective Services was spread out across various locations in the city, and it had taken Connor a good three days before he finally located the caseworker he hoped could help him. Navigating the tangle of bureaucracy was exhausting, and he'd been challenged each step of the way. One caseworker accused him of wanting to cause the child trouble, and no amount of reassurance seemed to calm her down. It'd taken a supervisor and a call from his command officer to finally get the name of someone who could possibly point him in the right direction.

Now it was a matter of seeing if he'd found the right caseworker or if she was just another stop along the way.

"Come in," a cheery female voice called out to him. "Mind the boxes at the door, though."

Opening the door farther, Connor squeezed in, careful not to get his equipment belt caught on the knob. Hunting down social workers had become a part-time job of sorts, shaving a few hours off his shifts by agreeing to be on call while he roamed the seemingly endless governmental halls. Stepping carefully around a tower of boxes, he searched for someplace safe to stand in what looked like a tornado-struck office space anchored by an old metal desk and a broadly smiling older woman dressed in a floral cotton shift, her tousled short brown curls touched with a bit of silver and various magenta streaks. A pair of wire-rimmed glasses were perched on her nose, fingerprints streaking the lenses, but the twinkle in her warm eyes was as clear as day.

"Hello, Lieutenant." She leaned forward from her place behind the desk, squinting at his uniform insignia. "I got that right, yes? Your rank?"

"Yes, ma'am," Connor responded, returning her smile. "I'm hoping I have the right office. I am looking for a Ms. Stice. I'm Lieutenant Connor Morgan. I was hoping to talk to you about a Social Services case that you might be in charge of."

"Call me Kathy." She gestured at an office chair half buried under a stack of papers. "Please feel free to move those and have a seat. One of my coworkers just retired, and apparently they needed the office space very badly because someone just packed everything up and dumped it here. So I am going through things and discovering he was bit of a packrat. I don't think we need twenty years of health bulletins about the common cold and how to avoid it."

"If you like, I can find a metal trash bin and you can have a spontaneous bonfire," he suggested, chuckling along with her when she laughed. "Strange things happen in old buildings. I'm sure it'd be fine if I just stood by with a fire extinguisher so things don't get out of control."

"I might take you up on that." Waving an empty manila folder in the air, she shook her head. "We do so little on paper nowadays, I'm shocked they still make these. But let's not take up too much of your time. What can I do for you?"

"A few weeks ago during one of our operations, I pulled a little boy out of a drug house." Connor eyed the chair, not trusting it to support him, so he stayed on his feet. "There was a young woman in the room with him, possibly his mother. She was deceased before we made entry. Coroner called it as an OD. As far as I know, the boy ended up with CPS."

The jovial grandmotherly smile disappeared, replaced by an assessing, steady look. Rolling her chair back, the caseworker set aside what she'd been shuffling through, her attention fixed on Connor's face. "I think I know the case you're talking about. My question is, why are you asking after him? Do you think he has some kind of information about what was going on in that house? Because if you do think that, there are channels for that kind of inquiry, unless you're on a fishing trip and don't really know what you're looking for."

"Nothing like that, ma'am." He shook his head, shifting his weight off his booted foot. "This is going to seem a bit unorthodox—maybe even a little bit crazy—but there was something about him that… I don't know why, but handing him over to the caseworker on the scene felt like I was abandoning him. It's been bothering me ever since, and I've had several long talks with my husband about it."

"What kind of talks?" She frowned slightly, pushing her glasses farther up the bridge of her nose. "I'm not sure what you're getting at."

"I don't know if he has family that's taking him in." Another shift of his foot and he caught a pile of papers with his right hand before they tumbled to the floor from their precarious position on a nearby box. "We wanted to see if it was possible to foster him, maybe even adopt him if things work out that way, but it just feels like the world has thrown him away, and nobody deserves to grow up thinking that. Especially not him."

"I am curious about something, Lieutenant Morgan. Why this little boy?" The caseworker asked, plucking a pen out from an ink-marked mug sitting on her desk. "What made you and your husband decide to take him in?"

It took Connor a minute to gather his thoughts. They scattered when he tried to focus on a single reason for wanting to open his home and heart—his family—to the terrified little boy he rescued from a firefight. Words became fleeting clouds swept away by the overwhelming winds of his emotions, so Connor gave in to the confusion churning within him and replied with the first thing that came to mind, "I don't know."

Ms. Stice's eyebrows rose.

"It took me a while to sort out the uneasiness I felt when leaving him," he admitted softly, hooking his thumbs into his pants pockets and letting his attention drift as he sifted through his thoughts. "I spoke to a couple of family members before I talked to Forest—my husband—about it, because I wasn't even sure if I should bring it up to him. But the idea of this kid being caught up in the foster care system with as little as I know about it makes me sick to my stomach, and Forest knows what it's like to be a kid caught up in that red tape.

"He doesn't want that for anyone and… we just spent a lot of time talking and neither one of us wanted to abandon him to that." Connor cleared his throat. "Maybe I feel connected to him because I see a little bit of Forest in him, and I can't undo what my husband experienced but we're hoping we could change the future for one little boy. Give him a home. Make him feel safe. And when he's grown, hopefully we've done a good enough job for him to go out to make the world a better place for someone else."

CHAPTER FIVE

"HAVE YOU heard anything from that caseworker? How long has it been? Four? Five months?"

Normally Connor didn't mind his younger brother tagging along with him to observe other tactical teams as they went through a training course, but as much as he loved Kane, sometimes the SFPD inspector was as much of a pain in the ass as he had been when they were kids. Standing on a platform with a clear view of the roofless house the department used for training, Connor estimated the potential two-and-a-half story drop would result in seriously injuring Kane if he chucked his brother over the railing.

The team currently running the course was disorganized, and despite having muted his communication headset, their training officer was running hot and vocal, yelling loud enough to be heard clearly despite being at the other end of the long warehouse the training modules were set up in. One of the officers, a fresh-faced blond woman with her features buried beneath protective gear, was clearly as disgusted by her team as their TO. Slumped against an interior wall, she was shaking her head as the rest of her team members were being picked off by Connor's team posing as hostiles residing in the small structure.

"I'm only asking because Miki was talking about it last night." Kane leaned his forearms on the railing Connor knew he could toss his younger brother over if he had enough leverage. "Unless you guys fucked something up and there is no way in hell CPS would give you a goldfish, much less a kid."

"We didn't fuck anything up," Connor said between his gritted teeth. "We passed with flying colors on everything—good school, a solid support system, a bedroom with a connecting bathroom. If anything, the two they sent over to inspect the house recognized Forest and spent more time talking to him about the band instead of taking a look around. I could have had a torture rack in the living room and I think they would have just figured it was something he used on stage."

"So you've heard nothing."

"Not in the last few days since Mum asked me." He winced when one of his newer recruits sliced a stream of paintballs across a pair of the responding team's officers, marbling their bellies with bright splatters. For a moment he thought the taller of the two was going to argue about his ignoble death, but considering he had to look up into Browning's face shield, he took the wise route and flopped down, play-acting as one of the many bodies in the building. "God, this is a bloodbath. Matt said this team was ready, but it doesn't even look like they know which end of the gun their ammo comes out of."

The squad looked forward to training days with rookies, gleefully plotting on how to work the missions they were assigned. The walls of the fake house were movable, so they never knew what configuration it would be in, much like an actual raid. But playing the bad guy had its perks, and the exercises served as training, even for his most experienced officers. With his foot healed up and with the clearance to return to full duty, Connor had been looking forward to running the course, even with Kane watching from one of the upper platforms. He'd taken two of the missions, and small daubs of white paint were caught in the creases of his pants, blowback from a hit Yamamoto took five minutes into the first session.

"You remember being this young?" Kane mused. "I swear to God it was just last week. Sure you're spry enough to chase after a kid?"

"I can catch you," Connor shot back. "And yeah, it's frustrating that we haven't heard anything, but at least we know he's in the system, and maybe he's doing really well where he is. I don't know. I feel like I got Forest stirred up over nothing, even though we had some really good talks about it... about a lot of things. That was something really great that came out of this. We know that we both want kids, and it really doesn't matter where they come from, because they'll be ours."

"Still thinking about doing the martini shaker with Kiki's eggs?" Connor caught Kane's quickly suppressed grimace. "With your luck, you'll get Mum's clone and she'll think it's a sign to start building her army."

"She already had her chance, and the only one that came out like her is Kiki," he pointed out with a laugh. "It's still on the table. Everything is kind of still on the table."

"Well, don't wait too long," Kane warned. "You don't want to be attending your kid's high school graduation and fall asleep in your chair because it's past your bedtime."

Connor waited a beat, then said, "You know, you and Miki could have a kid. Maybe even two."

The withering look Kane gave him could probably have been felt by the rookie team below them who were coming under fire again.

Shaking his head, Kane muttered, "I'm pretty sure that the species Miki came from eats its own young. And I'd be right there with him, ready for the chili crisp and shoyu if he needed it."

"They are about to call this one over." Connor reached down to pick up his helmet from the floor. "Want to gear up and join in on the next one? It might give the rookies a fighting chance if you're running on our side."

"Screw you." Kane snorted. "Give me five minutes, and then I'll show you how it's done."

"RAFE, I'M not saying you might be in the wrong time signature," Damien's slightly British accent delivered his words with a sharp, choppy flow. "But it sounds like you're not even playing the right song. Maybe you want to catch up with the rest of us?"

"Maybe you're on the wrong song," Crossroad Gin's bassist shot back. "I'm following along with the drums, and Forest is always on pace. What are you playing?"

Their banter was a friendly normal that Forest welcomed. Each member of the band had his own role. Miki wrote nearly all of their music but got input from the others and listed everyone as a songwriter, giving each band member an equal share. Under Damien's leadership, they navigated through a growing catalog as he managed their relationship with their record company alongside Edie, their band coordinator. Rafe served as a braking mechanism of sorts, smoothing out some of their songs' rougher edges and providing a fun-loving, charismatic stage presence in contrast to Miki's sensual aloofness. Forest had wondered how much he actually contributed, until they all went out on the road and he realized he was the only one of the four band members with a lick of common sense.

A common sense that probably helped them stay out of jail more than a few times while working their way across the country playing those small gigs.

Now, with most of the tracks written and rehearsed for their next album, talk about touring again had kicked up, and this time, the audiences would be in the thousands. Every time Forest thought about it, his stomach twisted up in knots, but his trepidation wasn't as strong as the growing excitement of sharing a large stage with three of his best friends.

Even if the lead guitarist and bassist couldn't seem to agree about what they should have been playing.

"How about if we take a break?" Miki cut through Rafe and Damien's chatter. "Something with this isn't working, so maybe I've got to go over it again. I probably fucked something up and didn't copy it right."

They all had egos, even Forest. Music was something that bound them together, but they all knew from experience that compromise was going to be the only thing that kept them that way. The more fiery arguments were usually between Damien and Miki, artistic souls with different views but mindful of the band's signature sound. The foundation of their music was rooted too deep in the blues, but like much of rock, influenced by their own experiences and other musicians. Having played in the studio for a variety of different styles and genres, Forest brought with him a wider exposure to varying sounds, but he'd found a soulmate of sorts in Miki, who drank in practically every bit of music he heard, from classical to Chinese opera.

And sometimes, those influences snuck into their compositions, smacking Damien and Rafe from seemingly out of nowhere.

The arguing was playful, a light teasing about who was the better musician, with Miki rolling his eyes at each outlandish boast. After unfolding himself out from under his drum kit, Forest stretched, his shoulders and spine crackling back into place. From his perch at the end of the love seat, Dude looked up, then yawned, clearly bored with the band and its playing.

"Where's your music?" Miki asked, looking up at Forest from a pile of papers. "Let me see if I got yours right."

"I'm going to have to dig it out," Forest replied. "I was playing from memory."

"Of course you were," Rafe sneered, no heat in his voice other than a suppressed chuckle. "Teacher's pet. You know, you were the kind of kid whose head got flushed down the toilet during school."

"They could have tried." He returned Rafe's good-natured smirk with a toothy smile. "Unlike you, I didn't have a pack of Morgans to protect me, so I had to make sure I was the last person they wanted to do that to."

Ignoring the verbal fallout of his remark when Damien picked up his teasing again, Forest dug into the backpack he'd shoved his notebooks into. Crouching over, his face was well within Dude's tongue range, and he almost toppled over when the dog sneaked a lick across his face.

"Dude, watch the mouth. You do some disgusting things with that tongue there." He was about to grab his music sheets when his phone chirped at him from the depths of the pack. Glancing over his shoulder, he saw the other three still engaged in their not-so-serious argument about the song they'd been playing, so he answered his phone. "Hello?"

The moment he heard what the woman on the other side of the line had to say, Forest half wished he'd ignored the call so his world wouldn't be turned upside down.

"No, I can be there in probably half an hour, maybe more if there's traffic." His mind was scrambled, a thousand things popping up in rapid succession. He couldn't remember if he'd put gas in his SUV or why Connor wasn't answering his phone. Clutching the musical notations he'd found, a spark of clarity had his arm gesticulating frantically at Miki, silently begging his friend to take the papers and relieve him of something—anything—so he could clear his brain. "I'll try to get a hold of my husband. He's probably in a meeting or something. I'll see if I can get him to meet us there."

There was more information, an address he repeated back to the officious-sounding woman with her harried, clipped voice slicing through what sounded like chaos going on around her. It was hard to hear her above an escalation of shouting, and Forest waited a moment before asking her to repeat what she said.

"Just bring your identification with you, Mr. Ackerman." Her words came at him in a rapid-fire stream. "I've got other calls to make. Someone will see you down at the facility. They'll fill you in when you get here."

Forest found himself listening to dead air. The call had ended abruptly without any reassurances that he would survive what lay ahead of him. He realized he was still crouching and within tongue range of a now concerned blond terrier. The papers were gone from his hand and the butterflies in his stomach were now ice shards, digging down into his guts and churning away. His bandmates were standing over him, a semicircle of worried faces and loyal friendships. Standing up seemed to take every ounce of effort he had, but it was the next step in what he had to do, even if he just wanted to bury his face into Dude's fur and forget about the phone call he just got.

"What happened?" Always their leader, Damien stepped in, reaching for Forest's backpack on the floor. "You look like you've seen a ghost, man."

"She didn't give me any of the details, but I have to get down to some place near Central," he stuttered, staring down at his phone for a moment. Then he texted an emergency code for Connor to call him back. Belatedly, Forest remembered the training exercises Connor's squad volunteered for and the reminder he'd been given that there would be gaps in the day when Con was away from his phone. "Something shitty happened. I don't know what, but they want us to come down there and take home that little boy."

"WE'LL BE right outside if you need us," Miki reassured Forest, patting him on the shoulder. "I'm sorry one of us can't go with you—"

"No, no," Forest said, nodding. "It's okay. It makes sense for privacy and everything. I appreciate you guys coming down here. I really do."

"As soon as Connor gets here, we'll tell him what he needs to do and send him in," the singer promised. "Damie texted me while you were finishing up some of the paperwork. He's coming back with a car seat, and he and Rafe are going to try to get it installed in your back seat. I got the keys, so hopefully by the time you're done, it'll be already for you to go."

There'd been so much information thrown at him, and Forest could only nod again, stuck in some kind of loop where his only response was acquiescence. The caseworker who'd done his intake surprised him with a list of things he had to have ready prior to Social Services releasing the new member of their family. The inclusion of the car seat brought him up short, and Damien intervened, promising the young woman he would go out and get one so the little boy didn't have to remain in the facility.

"No one said anything about needing a car seat," Forest mumbled under his breath at Miki. "You'd think someone along the way would've said something. Suppose Damie hadn't been here? What if I was by myself?"

"Just be glad it's only a booster seat," Miki reminded him. "I've heard horror stories about people trying to install car seats to bring their kids home from the hospital. Pretty sure a few of them just give up and live in the parking lot until the kid can walk."

"What happens if he hates me?" The idea sprung into his head, stuck to the side of his skull like a stain Forest couldn't get rid of. "I don't know what the fuck I'm doing."

"Nobody does, dude." He gestured at the large, noisy area they'd walked into nearly two hours ago. "You can't fuck it up worse than what anyone did to us, right? And it's not like you're going to be alone. We've got you. Connor's crazy family has your back. No matter what you need, one of us will make it happen."

"Even if the kid wants ice cream at two o'clock in the morning?" Forest grinned, recalling a time when Miki badly wanted an ice cream sandwich in the middle of the night when they were on tour.

"Just give me a call," Miki replied. "I'll send Kane out to get you some."

Waiting was the worst part of it. The address they'd arrived at turned out to be a community center commandeered by an army of social workers and police officers. An activity area at the front of the building served as a reception-intake space, a long counter manned by a few caseworkers cutting off access to a pair of hallways leading to the back of the facility. By Forest's count, there appeared to be at least eight or nine other foster parents waiting for a child to be processed. The caseworker who'd called his name hadn't been able to give a lot of information, citing an ongoing investigation, but the worry in his expression was enough to give Forest pause.

An older woman with a toddler on her hip ambled by, carrying on a phone conversation about what could be made for dinner and that she didn't know how long she would be. From what Forest could gather, her family would be making room for two children, sisters who'd been taken out of what CPS considered a dangerous living situation. Whoever she was talking to said something amusing, because her soft laughter made the child she was holding giggle. After promising she would call if it got too late, she hung up her phone, then blew a raspberry on the toddler's chubby cheek, making it laugh harder.

"Ackerman?" A broad-shouldered policewoman stood at the end of the reception counter, her fingers tapping on the back of a clipboard she held clenched in her hands. "Do you know when your spouse will be here? They need to go over a few things with the both of you before the child can be released."

"He said he was only a few minutes out when I texted him last." Forest checked his phone again, not seeing an update for Connor's ETA. "I can give him a call if—"

"No need," Miki interrupted. "He just got here."

Connor came through the double doors of the community center as if a dragon was on his tail. Even stripped down to the bare basics of his uniform, tactical belt and weapons removed, the stark black of his clothing and boots shouted authority. Scanning the room quickly, his cop face stern and calculating, Connor's narrowed blue eyes swept over everyone around him, then settled on Forest, standing on the far side of the space. His long stride quickly shortened the distance between them, the soles of his boots striking the cheap tile floors with resonating thumps. Reaching Forest's side, Connor nodded once at Miki, then brushed his lips over Forest's temple.

"You might want to tone that cop shit down, Con," Miki drawled. "You're here to pick up a foster kid, not looking for a dogfight."

Connor inhaled sharply as if to argue with Miki; then he visibly relaxed. Bleeding off the tenseness in his body language, he shook his head in a silent acknowledgment of Miki's comment. The female cop's hand drifted away from her weapon belt, picking up the clipboard she'd placed down on the reception desk when Connor came in.

"Sorry." Connor shot the police officer an apologetic smile. "I just got off the phone with the inspector leading this case. I didn't mean to come in that hot."

"We just need to verify your identity. Then I take you both back." The officer glanced down at the SFPD star affixed to Connor's belt. "Sorry, Lieutenant. I didn't see your badge, sir."

"No, that's on me," Connor replied. "I didn't have a lanyard in the car. I've got ID on me. Just let me get cleared with the intake people and we can go back. I know they need to talk to us."

"Do you know what happened?" Chewing his lower lip, Forest wondered what he was getting into, and that sinking feeling reached new depths when Connor nodded. "Are we going to be able to do this?"

"Yeah." His husband's expression softened as he squeezed Forest's hand. "I think we are going to be the best thing for him. I'll be right back."

"Is Kane outside?" Miki called after Connor as he began to walk toward the intake caseworker.

"Yeah, he's in the parking lot with the two idiots you sent to get a car seat," the eldest Morgan replied. "You might want to go check on them. I don't know how they did it, but they somehow installed it upside down."

THE HALLWAY seemed to stretch on endlessly, and Forest was beginning to think he had somehow fallen down a rabbit hole and they were on their way to a Mad Hatter's tea party. The officer leading them was quiet the entire way, and the stillness at the back of the building—such a contrast from the babble of chaos at the front—was disconcerting. Even the comfort of Connor's hand in his didn't seem to keep the shivers of anticipation from tickling Forest's spine. Finally, they reached a door and the officer opened it and ushered them in.

Forest didn't know what he expected, but it certainly wasn't a small darkened room with one wall dominated by a smoky tinted window. A curvy woman with keen cop eyes leaned against a narrow table shoved up against the wall opposite the window, her attention dragged away from the room on the other side of the glass when they walked in. She looked to be in her midthirties, her dark hair cut into a shaggy bob, and her black jeans and long leather jacket were typical of an inspector who worked the streets, the ball chain hanging from her neck pulled down her chest with the weight of her SFPD badge. She moved forward, her jacket swinging away from her waist, a glint of her weapon peeking out as she stood.

"You got here faster than I thought, sir." Holding out her hand for Connor, she continued, "I'm Inspector Suppes. We spoke on the phone."

"Please, call me Connor. I'm not here as a cop. This is my husband, Forest." He turned, releasing the inspector's hand so Forest could shake it. "They didn't give him any information up front, and I don't have the full story."

"We don't even know his name," Forest said, moving more into the room. It dawned on him the window was actually a one-way mirror, and once he stepped in, he had a clear view of what was going on in the larger room beyond. What he saw shocked him speechless.

He didn't know what he was expecting, but it certainly wasn't the triage setting of medics and cops working on nine children of various ages sitting on hospital beds and cots. Hovering near each child was what Forest assumed were social workers, all of their voices muted by the thick glass. A speaker set into the wall of the small room was obviously turned off, but he could feel the children's distress as loudly as if it blared out every word being said.

Connor tapped Forest on the shoulder, then pointed to a wide-eyed frightened little boy sitting to the left side of the larger room. "That's him over there."

The boy's dark hair was cut into jagged shanks, long chunks partially obscuring his lean face, but enough of it showed for Forest to see the dark bruises and thick swelling along his cheeks and jaw. His lower lip jutted out on the right side of his mouth, dried blood dotting a split running diagonally over his flesh. He'd wrapped his thin arms around himself, leaning away from the woman crouching in front of him, her mouth moving silently, and whatever she was asking, he shook his head and looked away.

A quick look around the room told Forest the other children were in as bad or worse shape—a little girl not more than two or three sporting a pair of casts on her arms while a toddler wailed loudly as an EMT plucked the remains of a torn, bloody shirt from a wound on his back. Next to him, he felt Connor tense up and growl, a rumbling, protective sound he'd heard more than once from a few Morgans in the past.

"He's not nonverbal, per se, but he sure as hell doesn't say a lot," Inspector Suppes murmured. "The woman you found next to him turned out to be his mother. Every family member we located for her is either dead or in jail. She didn't give birth to him in a hospital, so his record of birth is a bit sketchy because she filed it when he was about three or four. He's nearly eight now, going off what information she gave."

"What's his name?" Forest asked. "For some reason, everyone we ever talk to about him wasn't willing to tell us."

"His name on record is Tate Robinson." She nodded when Connor let loose with a low, hissing Gaelic curse. "I didn't understand what you said, but I can guess. He's the son of the man your team raided that day, and as for what happened to him and the other kids? Either his father wants him back or his enemies want to use him for revenge."

CHAPTER SIX

"WHAT CAN you tell us about the investigation?" Connor joined the inspector, resting his hip against the table while he watched the caseworker speak to Tate. The young boy's eyes shifted, taking in the whole room without once landing on the woman talking to him. "What happened to him?"

Forest stood silently before the one-way mirror, his thumbs hooked into his front pockets and his somber face reflected back in the glass, his expression flat except for the glimmer of moistness in his doe-soft eyes. The inspector gazed at Forest for a moment, then turned her attention to Connor.

"Neighbors next to a duplex were getting concerned about some of the noises they heard coming out of a common area in the back. They called it in to the station, and a patrol swung by, hoping to talk to someone and see what was going on." She shifted slightly, moving her weight from one foot to the other. "It was just bad luck, or maybe good luck, that they got there a few moments after some thugs from the Young Kings showed up."

"YK and Robinson have been battling for territory for almost a year now," Connor murmured. "Most of what my squad deals with is gang-related, but this is the first time I've heard about one of them going after a kid."

"They weren't after him. Or at least not at first," the inspector continued. "Both duplexes were residence homes for foster kids, but CPS had them on a watchlist because they suspected they were letting some of the kids' parents drop by when there are no-contact orders in place. In a way, the two sets of foster parents were double dipping. They got money from the state for the kids, and for enough cash, they would look the other way if you had a protective order against you and wanted to drop by to discourage your kid from telling stories about you. The people who lived next door moved on and a new family came in—a very curious and well-meaning family—who were kind of alarmed by how banged up the kids looked."

"What the hell good is a watchlist if no one's watching?" Forest grumbled from his sentinel post in front of the mirror. "I hate CPS. So fucking useless."

She glanced again at Forest, her eyebrows knitted into a frown. "Is he okay?"

"Former foster kid." He wanted to reach out and touch Forest, pull him from whatever thoughts he was having, but Connor wasn't sure if it would help. The stiffness of Forest's shoulders and the firm line of his spine was enough of a tell for Connor to read his anger. "He did better out of the system than inside of it."

"I think that's true for a lot of kids," Suppes agreed. "To make this long story short, apparently one of Robinson's guys—a drug runner named Scott Walker—somehow found out where the kid was and took it upon himself to see if Tate talked about anything he saw."

"Did Walker think the kid was taking notes about Robinson's drug deals?" Connor shook his head. "What did he think the boy could tell us?"

"I don't know. One of the older kids was in the room when Walker started asking questions. When Tate didn't respond, that's when Walker began hitting him. By then, the neighbors had already contacted the nearby station. The YK guys showed up about two minutes before the responding patrols arrived, and that's when things all went to hell." The inspector swept her gaze across the occupants beyond the mirror. "The YK posse knew Walker on sight. Our boys in blue pretty much walked into a gunfight.

"When it was all said and done, Walker and one of the YK guys were dead, the senior officer took a hit to his leg, and CPS finally decided that maybe the duplex wasn't a good place for the kids to be," she growled, gripping the table tightly. "That's when we moved the kids over to Central. Stice took control of their cases and started doing some dialing. Social Services isn't too happy with us, but I have a lot more confidence in the caseworkers on our end of the city. I don't know what they've got planned for that other office—"

"I can think of a few things," Connor cut her off. "They're just... he's a little kid. They're all just... *kids*."

He'd known what he was facing before he put on an SFPD uniform, and even then the horrific things people did to one another... to children... surprised the hell out of him. There'd been more than one call when he left the scene wondering if he should turn in his star and walk away from all of the violence and darkness he waded through every day.

"Did those people have him all this time?" Forest's soft voice was threaded hard with anger. "Is that where he's been living? Where somebody can just walk in and beat the shit out of him?"

"I don't know," Suppes confessed. "I haven't read any of the kids' case files. I only got notice about the Robinson connection because he's one of my suspects in a burglary ring. We knew his girlfriend had been found dead after a SWAT raid, but my partner and I didn't find out about the kid until today. There is no evidence Robinson's involved in the boy's life, other than keeping his mother around. According to what little CPS knows, he hasn't shown any interest in getting the boy back or even seeing him. The court records Tate as abandoned, so that's how Central CPS is treating him."

"Looks like the caseworker is done," Connor said, standing up. "What else do we need to do in order to get him out of here?"

"She'll probably want to talk to you and give you a breakdown about how he is," the inspector replied. "Mind you, she's only had a few hours with him, and like I said, that office's paperwork is suspect, so none of us here are putting a lot of weight behind it. Stice divided up all of the cases among everyone under her, but there's a lot to go through, and you all are going to play catch-up."

There was a brief knock on the door, and then the caseworker they'd seen speaking to Tate let herself in. A tall woman with generous curves, she smiled wearily at Connor and Forest, then sighed as she shut the door behind her. Her vividly colored paisley shirt and worn jeans gave her an approachable, comfortable look, her dark blond hair a bit of a frizzy mess and held back from her face by a headband that matched her tortoiseshell glasses. The narrow room was a tight fit, but not as uncomfortable as Connor imagined it could have been if Tate's original caseworker had come through the door.

"Hello, I'm Petra Williams." Her soothing voice rolled over them, and her handshake was firm as she greeted everyone. Clutching a thick folder to her chest, she settled into a corner of the room, facing Connor and Forest. "I'm sorry to have made you wait, but I wanted to get a good idea about how he was feeling. I needed to be able to give you an idea about what you might be dealing with and touch base with you to see if you were still on board with taking him in."

"We are as sure as hell not leaving him," Connor asserted. "Run us through what we need to do and we'll get him home."

"Let me do a quick rundown with you now, but I'll also give you a case file with all of his pertinent information to take with you. That includes all of his medical records and educational assessment. He should be enrolled in school as soon as possible, but please keep in mind, he hasn't had a lot of exposure to that environment, so it's going to be rough going." Offering the folder she held to Forest, the caseworker continued, "He's in relatively good health but still slightly malnourished. The psychiatrist who spoke with him says Tate is extremely bright but not very communicative. Definite signs of physical and emotional abuse. She doesn't think he was taken advantage of sexually, but she wants to continue to work with him to assess him on that, just in case. Right now, he doesn't volunteer a lot about what he's feeling, but that's understandable, considering he hasn't had a responsive or stable home environment."

Watching Forest's expressions as he read Tate's file called up a flood of emotions for Connor. The few times Forest was willing to speak about how he grew up and the things he'd gone through were usually in the dead of night, when the shadows were pulled up against their bed and only a faint bit of light reached through the curtains from somewhere beyond.

He intimately knew the landscape of Forest's body—the sleek tautness of his muscles and long limbs, but also the odd imperfections on his smooth skin. Connor once asked about the small circular scars above one of Forest's knees, only for his husband to shut down and look away. There were other dark patches and minute keloids along his back and legs, but the circumstances had to be perfect and safe for Forest to share how they got there. There was a lot he didn't know about Forest's past, but Connor mourned the damaged little boy hidden deep inside of the man he loved unconditionally.

"Does he have anything that we need to take with us?" Connor pushed off the table, then walked over to his husband. Edging up against Forest's side, he read over the drummer's shoulder, skimming over what looked like an intake report. "Looks like he had a lice infestation. Did they clear that up, or is that something we need to take care of?"

"Nobody has brought anything over from the houses the kids were in," the caseworker replied. "I didn't see any infestation, but I can't say for sure. Two of the kids in the other duplex came in with lice. Medical hasn't given him an all-clear yet, but they're working on it."

"I know how to get rid of those." Forest glanced up and smiled at Connor's grimace and slight shudder. "Stuff like that happens. Choose between food and lice shampoo? I'd grab the Vienna sausage and some crackers, then see if I could get someone to shave my head. That's just how things were."

"Pretty sure they'll check before he's released," Suppes interjected. "That way you can stop by the store if you need to."

"Thanks. Hopefully he's clear. I'd hate for his first experience at the house to be a chemical bath. If he's not, then we'll deal with it," Connor murmured, continuing to read the file and nodding when Forest asked if he was done with one of the pages. "I wonder if he even remembers me."

"Con, you're nearly the size of a grizzly bear, and you yanked him out of a gunfight. Pretty sure he remembers you," Forest snorted. "You're not only hard to miss, you're kind of hard to forget. God knows, I tried like hell to do just that when I first met you, and look at me now, wearing your ring and wondering what kind of ice cream the kid likes."

THE SMELL struck Forest first. The air was sour with unwashed children and harsh antiseptics. Whatever the community center had been before, the bleak desperation and hopelessness it held remained stained in its walls. Like many government buildings used to serve the unfortunate, the space's cinder-block walls were overpainted with a coat of thick industrial green. The fossilized remains of shelf brackets and sealed-off pipe ends jutted out periodically, their features nearly buried by their latex carapaces. Holding the heavy door open for the caseworker and Connor, Forest scanned the room, looking for the little boy they had observed behind the glass.

Tate hadn't noticed them come in. Possibly the EMT asking him questions kept his attention occupied, but even from across the room, resignation possessed the shadows in his dark eyes. The boy stared off at some point over the medical tech's shoulder, his lips barely moving when he offered up a response. Forest knew the dull numbness living inside of Tate. He'd resided in that dreary oubliette for much of his childhood, surfacing out of its dank shadows to grab at whatever little light and hope he could, but those were rare moments. It took years for Forest to realize he had a voice, yet no one wanted to hear him, and he had absolutely no power over what happened to him, no right to exist except what he was given.

The pain of living occupied every second. It murmured its dark promises that whatever pain Forest was feeling would be amplified without warning. He'd spent every bit of energy he had trying to fold in on himself, making himself as small of a target—emotionally and physically—hoping he could somehow avoid notice. And there were times that, no matter what he did, no matter how hard he tried, someone's anger found him and he discovered new horrors he'd not known existed.

It was obvious to Forest that Tate existed in his own private hell and he was simply waiting for the next time someone struck out. Whatever the medical tech was saying, no matter how much comfort was offered, Tate's expression remained dead still. The only sign of life he gave was the occasional blink and the rattling shudder of his scrawny chest every time he took a breath.

Others from the reception area were escorted in, accompanied by someone from social services or a cop. The noise level grew into a hard, jagged murmur as people began to pepper their charges with what they probably thought were soothing tones, but anxiety rode all of their words, a Horseman not spoken about in any myth but just as savage as Death and War.

Ms. Williams was saying something, but Forest lost her words in the rising din of the room. Next to him, Connor stiffened; then his husband's large callused hand reached out and grabbed at Forest's fingers. The sharks in Forest's belly stopped gnawing on his insides, and he took a long, shuddering breath to calm himself.

"Are we ready for this?" he whispered to Connor, unable to take his eyes off the little boy they would be bringing into their lives.

"No." Connor cracked a wry smile. "But then, I don't think anybody is."

Something shifted in the room. Forest didn't know what it could have been. The children's fear reaching some unknown height, cresting into a traumatic break, or the arrival of strangers who would have control over their lives, orchestrating events and memories that would dig down deep inside of them, potentially leaving new wounds. There was no excitement in the room, no sense of homecoming or relief that someone safe was there. Pain and anxiety ran hot through the emotional tide crashing over everyone, regurgitating its familiar coppery taste in Forest's mouth.

And then Tate looked up.

His bruised face, etched deep with apprehension and hurt, changed so dramatically Forest wasn't sure it was the same child. His dark lashes were spiky with shed tears, and his expressive eyes glimmered, his gaze fixed on the man Forest loved. Hesitation stilled Tate until he resembled more statue than flesh. Then when Connor and Forest stepped toward him, he broke free from the emotional prison he'd put himself in.

"Morgan!" A single word—a joyfully struck bell in a chaotic storm of questions and sobs—rippled toward them, and then Tate was on his feet, shoving the medic aside. A sob broke from him, hiccupping gasps accenting every lunging step he took.

Then just as it had probably happened months ago, Tate was in Connor's arms, clutching the cop tightly because he knew his life depended on it.

"I got you, kiddo." Connor cradled the back of Tate's head as he rocked him, a hint of shock still on his face at catching the boy in midair. "It'll be okay. We're not going to let anybody hurt you."

Buried into the crook of Connor's neck, Tate was murmuring something, lost in a language Forest didn't understand, but he didn't need to. No one did.

Patting Tate's shoulder, Forest let out a small laugh when Connor smiled at him. "Since it looks like he remembers you, let's sign those papers and get out of here."

"I LEFT ALL of the clothes I brought in the boy's room. There are also a few different sizes of sneakers, because I didn't know what his foot length was. We can return whatever is too small." The tiny Irish warrior who'd given birth to eight strapping Morgans stared down into the saucepan she was stirring, small elbow pastas caught in a whirlwind of hot water. Her Emerald Isle accent was thicker than Connor's, her words rolling around in a soft lilt, affection woven through everything she said. "Do you have salad makings? You know how my boy is about vegetables. Do you think we have enough mac and cheese?"

Brigid flitted around the kitchen to rummage in the refrigerator. Standing by the sink, Forest leaned against the counter and watched his mother-in-law go through the produce he'd gotten the day before. He couldn't hear through the Victorian's thick walls, but he could imagine the conversation Tate was having with Connor. For someone tagged as uncommunicative, there had been a steady stream of chatter all the way home coming from the back seat, and it continued well into the house.

The garble of words—English mingled with spits of Korean and Spanish—only stilled when Donal stood up from the couch. Tate's eyes went from father to son, the Morgans' familial connection clearly stamped between them. When Brigid came out of the kitchen not more than a second later, his eyes grew wider and he took a step back and pressed himself into Connor's hip. For a brief moment, Forest feared Brigid would overwhelm Tate with her infectious energy, but instead she folded herself down into a crouch and held her hand out to him.

"Hello there, little man." Her riotous dark red curls tumbled around her pixie face, and her sweet smile held the promise of cookies and warm blankets. He tentatively took her hand, his shoulders lifting up slightly in an instinctive defense, but Tate met Brigid's gaze straight on. "How about you get a bath in, and when you're done, we'll have dinner?"

And just like that, Forest knew Tate had fallen in love.

"I don't know how much salad stuff we have, but there's frozen veggies," Forest offered. "I don't think Tate's going to be a big fan of anything green. Or at least I wouldn't have been. I can toss some bags of brussels sprouts into the oven and roast them. Connor likes them that way with butter or balsamic dressing."

"I couldn't get that boy to even look at them when he was small." Brigid found the frozen sprouts in the freezer and shook her head as she closed the door. "Kane and Quinn liked them, but you would've thought I was feeding Connor poison. There were quite a few times when the two brussels sprouts he refused to eat at dinner joined him for breakfast the next day. There was no convincing him that they were just like cabbage, which he loved."

"Let me help you with that." After turning the oven on to preheat, Forest retrieved a large baking sheet from one of the island's cabinets. He dumped the brussels sprouts onto the pan, sprinkled them with a bit of olive oil, then followed up with salt and bits of fried garlic. The domesticity he'd become accustomed to suddenly seemed outrageously odd, so far away from the nights he'd spent as a child crouched over something he'd stolen from the convenience store to eat for dinner.

"Are you all right, son?" Brigid touched the small of Forest's back. "Is the boy being here overwhelming you?"

He turned to face the woman he now considered his mother, and just like Tate had done to Connor hours before, Forest reached for her, blindly needing her to anchor him before he was swept away. Her hug was as fierce as her spirit, and Forest was left without any doubts Brigid would sacrifice everything for him.

"I've got you." The echo of Connor's words made Forest laugh, and Brigid stroked his hair. "You know you're not going to have to do this alone."

"I'm not sure why, but all of this is just bringing up a lot of bad memories, and that's got nothing to do with Tate," Forest said softly, straightening up out of Brigid's hug. "I'm more scared that I'm not going to be what he needs. That I'm somehow going to fuck him up like… my mom did to me."

Brigid reached up and cupped his face, forcing Forest to meet her intense gaze. "Now you listen to me, Forest Morgan Ackerman. If there is one thing you do well, it's loving the people you choose to have in your life. You are a blessing, not just to Connor, but all of us. Tate is lucky to have you, and you know firsthand some of the struggles he's had. You'll be able to speak for him for things that Connor can't, and you will show Tate those painful moments don't have to define him.

"You are as much my son as Connor is, and I know Donal feels the same way." Brigid reached up and tugged his left ear. "It's a very brave and risky thing the two of you are doing by taking a little boy in, but I have faith that he was put there in front of you for a reason. Not just to save his life, but maybe also to rescue you from the darkness you still keep inside of you sometimes. Maybe he's here to teach you how to let that all go. God knows, Forest, you deserve all of the happiness the world has to give you. You just need to accept it."

CHAPTER SEVEN

FOREST ALMOST didn't hear Tate come into the kitchen. The boy's light footsteps were partially masked by the spray nozzle's rushing jets hitting the baking sheet Forest was rinsing off. Glancing over his shoulder, he spotted the little boy lurking near the far end of the kitchen island, nervously shifting his weight from foot to foot. The bath had been good for him, and a few hydrocolloid bandages dotted his face and arms, covering his more serious scrapes and cuts. A darkening bruise had bloomed during the hours since they'd gotten home, and its vibrant edges seemed to be spreading out, angling toward his jaw, where another bruise curled down his neck. His rambling slowed during dinner and then stilled to an uneasy silence, tension stiffening his body language even when Brigid brought out ice cream.

"Are you my dad? Like, my *real* dad?"

Forest caught a spray of warm water on his face, Tate's question slamming into him unexpectedly. Turning off the nozzle, he reached for a dish towel to wipe his face, then mumbled at the boy, "Do you want to repeat that? I don't think I heard you right."

Tate shuffled farther into the kitchen, his expression wary and suspicious. He kept one hand firmly around one of the kitchen chair's backs, maintaining a barrier between himself and Forest. His solemn dark gaze remained fixed on Forest. It was obvious to the drummer that Tate was hyperaware of Forest's body language, reading every shift of weight and hand gestures. It was something Forest had forced himself to unlearn, but the habit still crept in now and again. The on-edge vigilance and reactive responses were behaviors he shared with Miki, ingrained pieces of trauma poured over them like concrete forms that were filled with rage or fear. Now it appeared that Tate was a member of that same club, and Forest was at a loss on how to put the little boy at ease.

So he sat on the kitchen floor, crossed his legs, and waited for Tate to respond.

Probably feeling a bit braver, Tate edged around the chair. "She told everyone Georgie is my dad, but he's not. I think she lied so he would give her money."

"Georgie? Oh, Robinson. So you think he's not your dad?" There hadn't been any evidence of Robinson being the boy's father except for the birth certificate filed long after Tate was born. Still, Forest couldn't understand how Tate would believe Forest was his father. "Why do you think it's me?"

"Because Mom had a picture of you and your friends on the wall at the last place we stayed at."

Forest couldn't figure out where Tate's mom could have gotten a photo of him. "A picture? On the wall?"

"Yeah, with some of your friends." He nodded, furrowing his brow. "It was pretty big. It covered up one of the holes in the wall Georgie made. One of the guys was there today. The one who kind of looks like a girl. I don't remember his name. But he went with a guy who looks like Morgan."

"I think you are going to have to stop calling Connor Morgan, because there's, like, a million of them named Morgan." Forest thought back to who was in the parking lot when they brought Tate out to the SUV. "Miki? He's got brown hair and light-colored eyes? Really nice voice?"

"I didn't hear him talk," Tate replied. "But he was in the picture too. You guys were all leaning against the wall that was painted with a dragon. And there was some graffiti around it."

The graffiti dragon snapped everything in place. At some point during the spring, their manager, Edie, had coaxed Damien into getting shots of the band to promote their last album, and they'd all dragged their feet on it. It had been impossible for them to all be in the mood at the same time to do it. When Miki invited a couple of tattoo artists they knew to have a go at the brick wall alleyway between his and Damie's warehouses, it seemed like as good of a time as any. The dragon was a gorgeous disjointed splash of color against the red brick and was still a little tacky when Forest leaned against its leg. It'd taken three days before he got the paint off his elbow, but the photos were good enough to satisfy Edie.

"I think that was a poster, dude." Forest leaned against the kitchen cabinet, shifting so its knob didn't dig into his shoulder blade. "Was there anything else on the wall, maybe? Other pictures?"

"Yeah. There was a picture of my mom and my uncle. He's in jail. Mom said he wasn't ever going to get out." Tate pursed his lips. "And there was a picture of a jaguar, but it was painted on fabric instead of paper."

Forest chuckled. "I think we all had that at some point."

"I thought maybe you sent Morgan to come get me. Because you were in that picture and then you came to get me." He sniffled, rubbing at his nose, then shrugged. "I wasn't sure, so...."

"I'm sorry, kiddo. But I'm not your dad." It broke Forest's heart to shake his head, but he knew where the kid might have gotten the idea. "I bet your mom listened to the music my band makes, and she just liked having a poster of us on the wall."

Tate sat down hard on the kitchen floor, then a moment later, mirrored Forest's position, biting his lip as he probably absorbed what Forest told him. Staring off at nothing, eventually he nodded his head and rolled his shoulders down, a dejected expression stealing over his features. "So you didn't send Morgan to come get me?"

"I don't know what happened in the universe that lined you up with Connor, but I can tell you we talked about what to do for very long time and both of us agreed to have you here with us," Forest began. "When they called us to come get you, I was really mad because they could have sent you home with us sooner, but they didn't. But you're here now, and all of us—all three of us—are kind of new at this family thing. Okay, Connor isn't, but I think you and I are."

"How long are they going to let me stay here?" Tate tilted his head.

There were agreements he and Connor made with the state before they had been allowed to take in Tate. First and foremost, there had to be no promise of a forever home or a permanent family. Someone from Child Services could knock on the door at any time and remove Tate from their household. He couldn't promise Tate anything, not even his next meal, and Forest ground his teeth in frustration, remembering the uncertainty of his own childhood and the instability of not knowing where he would sleep that night. Tate was already stained with the system's filth, and nothing Forest or Connor did would scrub it off. The foundation of distrust was already laid, and any shelter built on top of that would crumble with the next move.

"Con and I are going to fight to keep you here," Forest replied. "I'm going to fuck things up sometimes. Connor probably won't as much as I do, but he makes mistakes too. We're going to do our best. And no matter what happens, I can promise you that we are going to make sure you'll be okay."

"TATE ALMOST passed out while brushing his teeth." Forest closed their bedroom door behind him. He took a step, then turned the knob and opened the door a few inches. "That bruise on the side of his face is still swollen, so I think we need to have someone look at it tomorrow. I put some of that ointment your mom gave us on it, but I don't know."

It was always a pleasure for Connor to watch Forest wind down from his day, especially after things had gone sideways and they were alone. Around them, the old Victorian house settled, probably as exhausted as the men who owned it. There was a tightness around Forest's eyes, a sure sign of stress Connor recognized instantly. As his husband passed, Connor snagged Forest by the wrist and dragged him closer to the wide comfortable chair Connor lounged on. He was met with no resistance, and with a bit of deft handling, he got Forest nestled mostly in his lap, the musician's long legs draped over the chair's stuffed arm. Like the house, they sat still for a few moments, exhaling the fatigue trapped inside of them.

"I need a shower," Forest grumbled, but he made no move to get off Connor's lap. Leaning his back against the chair arm behind him, Forest sighed. "Today has been… a lot."

Connor bent his head down, nuzzling Forest's neck. He smelled faintly of hot dogs and a hint of masculine sweat, just enough to entice Connor into giving Forest's earlobe a quick bite. His husband let out a guttural hiss but didn't pull away.

"That tickles."

Connor repeated the nuzzle, then lightly bit the wet spot he'd left. "That's why I do it."

While he'd never thought he'd put a wedding ring on another man's hand, seeing the gold band on Forest's finger brought him more joy than Connor ever expected. He ran his thumb over the metal circlet, exploring the familiar landscape of Forest's callused hands. They'd made a very good life for themselves, and he'd upended it with the crazy idea of taking in a little boy they knew next to nothing about.

Connor had no regrets, but he also knew things were just getting started.

"What did the two of you talk about in the kitchen?" Connor quirked a grin when Forest snorted. "I was about to pop in, but it sounded really serious and I didn't want to interrupt."

"His mom had a poster of Crossroads on the wall. So he got it into his head that I must be his dad because why else would you have someone's picture up? You would have to be related, right?" Forest played with Connor's fingers, mimicking his husband's caress of their rings.

"But Robinson is his dad. Or at least on record."

"Tate says his mom listed Robinson as his father to get money out of the guy." After blowing a quick raspberry at Connor, Forest continued, "According to him, she hooked up with Robinson a couple of years after Tate was born. Don't know if that's true or not."

"Caseworker did say his birth certificate was filed a couple years after Tate was born instead of right away," he pointed out. "Could be Robinson isn't his father but we'd need a DNA test to determine that. Weird it wasn't done right away. You'd think the hospital would have taken care of that before she was released."

"Not everyone goes to the hospital to give birth, babe. My mom squatted in someone's RV and had me down at the beach." Forest snorted. "I didn't have a birth certificate until my mom found out she needed one to get me registered for school. She didn't put down anyone for my father but I guess she could have named anyone she wanted."

"Your mom's got a lot to answer for." Connor wanted to smooth away the tenseness in Forest's shoulders. "What did you tell Tate?"

"That I wasn't his father." He grimaced. "It felt like shit to say it, like I was slapping him in the face or something. He took it okay, but he was pretty quiet afterward."

"That could've been because he was so tired." Rubbing Forest's thigh, Connor began to sort through what seemed like a million questions crowding his thoughts. "The kid was beat up, caught in a gunfight between a bunch of drug dealers, ends up in a community center, then is handed off to a couple of guys he doesn't know. That is a long fucking day."

"Tomorrow is going to be just as long," Forest pointed out. "We've got to find a school to take him. He's got a lot of catching up to do."

"Quinn said he will hunt a good place down for us." He squeezed his husband's knee. "I am going to be really honest with you, babe, and tell you that I'm scared shitless about this. We've got a great support system with our family, and I know that we're going to make mistakes, but I just want this kid to feel safe."

"I don't think he's a kid anymore." Stretching his arms out in front of him, Forest shook his head. "When I was his age, school was the last thing on my mind. I was more worried about getting to the trash bins on the pier before anyone else so I could grab all the aluminum cans I could for money. Maybe we should take a couple of days and get him settled in, then fold school into the equation."

"That sounds smart," Connor agreed. "I talked to Leonard about taking a couple of weeks off so I can be here with Tate."

"Was he okay with that? Leonard, not Tate."

"Yeah, technically it comes out of my vacation time because it's not paternity leave. They won't grant that for a foster intake, but I've got more than enough hours to burn." Connor gave in to the urge to wrap his arms around Forest, drawing him in close. "Let's see where we all are after the weekend. Who knows? He might get really sick of us and want to go somewhere else."

"Really?" Forest leaned back, giving Connor a sharp side-eye. "Your mom let him have two bowls of ice cream after a very big dinner. That kid isn't going anywhere, Con. Not for a very long time."

THE SCREAMS began at three in the morning.

There was a high-pitched shriek, then the sound cut out as if someone unplugged a speaker. Connor sat up quickly and slid out from under the covers. Next to him, Forest mumbled and stirred, then cleared his throat, probably trying to shake the sleep off.

Patting his husband's leg, Connor said, "I'll take care of him. Go back to sleep."

"I don't want him to think I won't be there for him," Forest gently argued.

"How about if I go talk to him first?" he suggested in a soft whisper. "Maybe if you go down and get us all hot chocolate, I can have him settled down a bit and we can all talk."

"That sounds like a good plan." Forest reached for a T-shirt from the laundry basket of clean clothes neither one of them had put away. "I'll make the actual stuff instead of some packets, but don't be surprised if mine has a lot of whiskey in it."

Tate's bedroom was at the back of the house, a large space with its own bathroom and shaded by a bank of old trees. The hallway's wooden floors creaked in a few spots as Connor walked, and a slithering whimper crept out from the bedroom's partially open door.

"You okay, boyo?" Connor gave the door a quick rap with his knuckles. "Do you mind if I come in?"

He got a sniffle in response, so Connor pushed the door open and stepped in. Tate's pale face was tearstained, illuminated to a stark ivory from the soft glow of the streetlights outside. He was sitting up and trembling. A hard shudder rocked his slight body when Connor walked toward the bed, his knuckles white as he clutched the sheet draped over his legs. The boy visibly flinched when Connor drew near, pulling back away from the long dark shadow Connor cast in the ambient light.

Whatever nightmare Tate found that night rode him hard and left its mark on the boy's vulnerable psyche. His breathing was erratic, seemingly caught in his chest with every gasping breath, and he shrank back when Connor reached the side of the bed.

Back when he lived with his parents, Connor often found himself walking the halls to check on his younger siblings. Most slept restfully, but his younger brother, Quinn, too often carried the day's obstacles with him into his dreams. Connor couldn't count how many times he had sat with his baby brother until his terrors fled, sometimes going down the hall two or three times a night, sometimes alone, sometimes finding Kane already there. No amount of reassurance could bleed away the shame Quinn felt at being afraid of the world, and he'd often told his brothers he didn't need them there.

Connor knew better. He couldn't imagine the burdens Quinn carried, but he understood the fragile hold his younger brother had on his own emotions. Back then, Quinn lived day to day, keeping himself stitched together with established routines and murmured promises. The broken look he often wore in the middle of the night when his troubled shouts called Connor to his side was echoed on Tate's face. Battles had been fought in the shadows, uneven and overwhelming, with little regard to past traumas, and even as Connor dragged over a chair, Tate continued to fight the fragmented monsters plaguing him.

"I'm here, kiddo." He kept his voice low, falling into the same soothing tones he'd used to placate his siblings. "Forest is making us some hot chocolate. Do you want me to turn the light on a little bit? The lamp right here dims."

Tate let out a long exhale, the release shaking his chest. His gaze landed on Connor for a brief second, then drifted away, roaming about the room. There was enough light to see by, the room's long blackout curtains pulled back from the bank of windows on the rear wall, but Connor wasn't convinced that was strong enough to break Tate's attachment to his nightmare. Leaning over, Connor set the nightstand lamp to low, then returned his attention to the little boy still shaking beneath his bedding.

"Do you want to talk about it?" Connor ventured, still keeping his voice low. "I know for me, talking about things makes them less scary."

"You're never scared." Tate's retort was shaky but steeped in doubt. "You're huge. Nobody's ever going to hurt you. You could just bash their face and they'll leave you alone."

"It doesn't work that way. No matter how big you are, there is always going to be someone bigger," he explained. "And there are other ways to get hurt besides being hit. I get scared every time I go to do a job. Usually it's because I'm worried about anyone on my team getting hurt or if I can't rescue someone in time."

"Like me?" The boy's fingers flexed, gripping more of the bedding.

"Yeah, like you." Connor patted the bed, giving Tate a small smile. "But we got you out of there."

"Then why didn't you take me home right away? Why did I have to go to those other places?" Tate shifted in his bed, angling more toward the light. The room's shadows bled away but left behind the dark mottles bruising the little boy's face.

"First I had to talk to Forest about it. We needed to make sure that taking you in would actually help you. Then there was a lot that we had to do before CPS would even consider us." He gestured toward the rest of the room. "They had to make sure you had your own space and that we were good people."

"At Mrs. Christoff's place, we were all in one room." Tate tilted up his chin and frowned. "And Bobby was making meth in the shed."

"I'm not saying that CPS didn't make mistakes," Connor replied. "We did everything they asked us to, and then we never heard back. Not until today. But as soon as they called us, we got down there to take you home."

Tate's frown deepened. "How long are you going to let me stay here? I asked Forest, and he said you guys would fight CPS if they told me I had to go."

"That sounds about right." Connor rested his elbows on his knees. The day was still a few hours away, and Tate looked exhausted, but it didn't seem as if the little boy was ready to go back to sleep. "I wouldn't get into a fight with Forest. He is one of the easiest people to get along with, but if someone messes with somebody he loves, he makes sure they regret it. He's got your back. Both of us do."

"I'm sorry he's not my real dad."

"In a lot of ways, I am too, but sometimes there are people in your life who kind of become your parents even if they aren't related to you." A bit of Connor's heart brightened at the memory of Forest meeting Brigid for the first time. "You saw my mom and Forest today, didn't you? And my dad? They both really love him, and they're not his biological parents. If anything, sometimes I think my mom loves Forest more than I do because they have a lot in common."

"Is that a joke?" Tate regarded him suspiciously. "Because it sounds like it is."

"It is, but they do love him. And my mom really enjoyed meeting you."

"She kept feeding me," he conceded. "And Donal taught me a magic trick with a quarter."

"Yeah, he's really happy you're here. A whole new audience for the three magic tricks he knows."

Tate did another squirm under the sheets; then his expression dropped to a solemn mask. Not making eye contact with Connor, he said, "I keep having dreams about my mom trying to find me, but she isn't alive. She looks really bad, and it's like I know she's going to hurt me if she can grab me."

"You had a lot of bad things happen to you, and sometimes your brain can get confused. Then it takes someone or something you love and makes it bad because everything else around you doesn't feel good." He kept his attention on Tate, even though the little boy wouldn't meet his gaze. "As you start to feel better, you probably won't have that nightmare anymore, and if you do, we can get someone to help you get rid of it."

"I think I'm supposed to have that dream," Tate whispered. "I didn't take care of her. I didn't watch what she was taking, and she took too much. It's my fault. I should've paid attention. Now she's angry at me because she's dead."

Connor understood Tate's guilt. He'd asked so many of the same questions during Rafe's downward spiral with his first band. No matter what he and his family did or said, Rafe sunk deeper and deeper into his addictions, distancing himself from the Morgans and Sionn. Connor had been unwilling to accept the fact that he couldn't drag Rafe to sobriety, and there were times—very recently—when he still questioned if he could have done more. The guilt of failing one of his best friends shook Connor to the core, and when Rafe finally surfaced, Connor felt even more guilty for not fully trusting Rafe to remain sober.

It was easier now, but there were times when their friendship had been on edge. Now he was dealing with a little boy who'd mired himself in that guilt. The idea that the kid was responsible for his mother's death was outrageous, but Connor understood how Tate got there.

Now it was up to Connor to drag the boy out of that quicksand.

"I know you're probably not going to agree with me, but your mom dying isn't your fault. It might seem like that to you because you spent a lot of time trying to take care of her." Connor contemplated his approach, not wanting to demonize the dead woman he'd found with Tate. "Sometimes people do things that are very dangerous, and no matter what anyone says, they're still going to go and do it. They can't help it."

"The drugs?"

"Sometimes," he agreed. "Your mom might have even wanted to not do any drugs, but there was something inside of her that maybe made the world too crazy. I don't know. What I do know is you're not to blame for what happened. You didn't do anything wrong even if it feels like you did. And I get that. Forest probably does too. But that's something we can help you with, okay?"

"So you don't think she's mad at me?"

"No, kiddo. I don't think she's mad at you. I think your brain is just trying to work out how you feel, and we just need to remind it that all of that isn't your fault." Connor cocked his head at a series of faint squeaks in the hallway. "And I think that's Forest with our hot chocolate."

A burst of wind rattled one of the windows, and Tate jerked at the sound. The weather was picking up outside, battering at the trees. Connor stretched back to look outside at the backyard, not surprised to see fat droplets falling in random gusts. The heavy scent of rain seeped into the house, and then a hint of warm chocolate brushed it away when Forest came into the room with three steaming thick-walled mugs hooked skillfully through his fingers.

"You two still talking?" He crossed over toward the bed, then held out one hand to Connor. "Take the blue one first. If you want, I can leave you guys alone if that's what you need."

"That's up to Tate." The mug was hot, so Connor set it down on the nightstand before taking another out of Forest's grip.

"You can stay. Even if you aren't my real dad." Tate sniffed. "Nobody ever made me cocoa before whenever I had a bad dream."

"I think that's the best part about having family." Forest sat at the end of Tate's bed. "When things are going to shit, there's always somebody who's going to make you hot chocolate. And sometimes, that's all you need after a really crappy night."

CHAPTER EIGHT

IT WAS *almost* right. Forest didn't know what was wrong, but they were *so close* to being there.

And he knew in his gut that Miki felt it too.

A misty afternoon drizzle drifted over the old Victorian, another brush of chilled dampness moving across the Bay Area. The sporadic rainfall churned and ebbed, a common occurrence over the past few weeks. The sun seemed to be playing hide and seek with the clouds, teasing the wet hills with a splash of lemony beams, then whispering away under a cloak of icy gray droplets.

One of the greatest gifts Connor ever gave Forest was converting the large den at the back of the house into a music room. Double-glazed windows and thick soundproofing kept the sometimes caterwauling practice sessions Forest had with his bandmates contained within the house's firm plaster walls. It was a space for them to explore their thoughts or simply hang out, away from the more serious setup of their warehouse studio. The room's bay window with its padded seating was one of Miki's favorite perches, a few down-filled pillows set against the glass for him to lean on. The rain hitting the window finally grew heavy enough to set drops careening down the pane, and when Miki tilted his face toward the sky, they ran shadows over his cheekbones and jaw.

The blond terrier who'd moved into Miki's warehouse a few years ago lay stretched out on the rug. Dude's eyes were closed, and his feet were sticking straight up into the air, his paws dangling loosely. Letting out the occasional snore, the canine didn't seem to mind the barrage of music or the sporadic chats the musicians had at certain points of their creative process. A spit-gnarled tennis ball lay close to the dog's partially open mouth, one of the many toys Dude often brought along when he and Miki went wandering.

"It's crazy how quiet it is back here," the singer murmured, glancing at Forest through his long lashes. "With all the trees and flowers, you can't see the neighbors. It's like you guys are the only house on this hill."

"I'm pretty sure the neighbors are really happy that they can't hear me." Forest rolled a new drumstick around his fingers, testing its weight and feel. "I opened up some windows a couple of weeks ago, and I don't know where my brain was, but I forgot and left them like that when I finally figured out that transition I'd been working on. Connor got about five phone calls, wondering if he really had to hammer that loudly during *Jeopardy!*"

"Oh yeah, you were working with that large tambourin. Shifting time signatures are a bitch, and that thing gives off some pretty loud snaps." Miki tapped at the sheet music with the end of his pencil. "I can see how people would think it was a nail gun. What did Connor say? Did he throw you under the bus? I know how vicious the old people get around here."

"He took the blame for me. Although I don't know how he thought they would believe him, because there he was talking on the phone and I was back here still drilling away." Forest adjusted his feet on his drum kit's pedals. "Con and Tate were watching some action movie, so I guess they thought it was just part of the soundtrack. But yeah, five phone calls between him starting off in the living room and coming down the hall to find out what was going on. But that's on me."

"The kid doing okay, though?" There was an odd look on Miki's face, then he made a disgusted sound. "I remember the kids getting shuffled in and out. It was always this shit show. I know you guys are trying to make things work out with him. I mean, I hope that really happens, but you've got to know deep down inside he's waiting for somebody to tell him to pack up his shit because it's time to leave."

"I know what that's like," Forest confessed. "I think CPS and Frank had me more than my mom ever did. I think he's already past the point of believing us when we say we want to keep him here. I don't know what to do about that. Connor says it's just going to take time, but it kind of feels like he is living out of his backpack."

"Connor's not wrong." The singer shifted on the window seat, pulling his legs up and crossing them. "It's a lot of change, right? You were older, but you went through the same shit with Frank. You get so used to having to manage your own life, and then all of a sudden people move in on top of you. Next thing you know, there's times when you're supposed to eat and sleep with all of these obligations and responsibilities that don't make any fucking sense, but what choice do you have? You either go along with the flow, hope to ride it out, and figure out where you're going to land, or you push back on it, and they either try to break you or they throw you out."

"Yeah." The stool squeaked underneath him when Forest rocked back, fragmented memories caught in the amber of old arguments and abandoned dreams. "I know how that goes."

The first few fosters he had were run more like a business than a home, a clear divide between the couples' natural kids and the spare ones seemingly found in dumpster couches. Attending school was a mess, dropped into the middle of the school year with no understanding about what he was learning other than he couldn't seem to ever catch up. Even having not much to begin with, shifting to a new foster family often meant somehow losing half of his shit. Mostly everything he'd worn came from donation bins set up in a Social Services' back office, sometimes after an hour or two spent sifting through the castoffs looking for anything halfway decent amid the musty clothing. There was a certain smell a castoff child had, and Forest quickly recognized other fosters in the sea of children at every school he ended up in. He didn't want that for Tate. But for the life of him, Forest also didn't know how to promise a home to a little boy who could be ripped from their lives by a stranger's whim.

"Do you want to take a break? Maybe get something to eat?" Forest tried to brush off the cobwebs of bad memories with a shake of his hands to loosen up his tight muscles. "I've got a couple of laundry baskets I need to get upstairs, but then we can go digging for food."

"Very domestic. Very much married." Miki unfolded his long body from the window seat, setting down his papers and pencil on the cushions. "Who gets to wear the maid's outfit? You or Connor?"

"Like I can find a maid's outfit to fit Connor's shoulders." He scoffed. "And if I'm doing laundry for me, I might as well do all of it. The kid's clothes don't really take up that much room, and Connor pretty much wears only tactical uniforms, T-shirts, and jeans. You guys don't do each other's clothes?"

"Not really." Miki shook his head. "Okay, Kane grabs my stuff from the bathroom, but let's face it, he's the only one who uses the dresser and hangs up his clothes. I live out of the laundry basket by the closet. He does the whole 'separate colors and splash this thing on that spot.' I just shove everything into the washer, toss in one of those pod things, and hope for the best. It's better for his nerves if I don't wash his clothes. Better for mine too."

"Can you do me a favor and grab one of the baskets? That way I won't have to make two trips." His legs ached when he stood up, but Forest suspected some of the muscle strain was a result of Connor dragging him back into bed after dropping Tate off at school. "Just need to put the small blue one on Tate's bed. He'll put his own stuff up."

"Yeah, I can do that." Nudging Dude with the toe of his sneaker, Miki made a face at his dog when he got a grunt back from the canine. "Come on, Blondie. Grab your ball and let's go out to the kitchen. I don't trust you with Forest's drumsticks after the last time."

"You'd think after all these years, he'd stop taking things." Shuffling behind the singer and the grumbling dog, Forest closed the music room door behind him. "To be fair, I mean, they *are* sticks. Kind of dog-plaything shaped. I can't hold that against him."

"I can." Miki stepped around the slow-moving dog. "He's been doing that shit ever since Damie gave him a treat to get back a mic he picked up in the studio. If you're going to reward Dude for handing something over, he's going to keep taking shit. I love Damie, but he's got a dog scamming him. It's fucking embarrassing."

IF IT wasn't for Dude, Forest wouldn't have found what Tate hid under his bed. Or at least not before it became a biohazard.

"Dude, watch where you're going." Forest sidestepped around the scampering terrier, shifting the small laundry basket to his other hip. "And now Miki's got me talking to you like you understand me."

"He understands more than you think," Miki called out from the main bedroom. "It's crazy how he knows the difference between the sound of the opening up a bag of chips or a packet of ramen."

"Honestly, Dude," Forest muttered at the small dog. "I'm surprised he refused to eat uncooked noodles, considering how long you've been around him munching on them."

There was something comforting about clean clothes. He didn't know why, or maybe he just didn't want to look to close at the *why*, but the fragrance of soap and fabric softener touched something rough lying in Forest's soul, soothing the jagged edges left by too many years of nasty memories. Bumping Tate's door open with his shoulder, Forest got another whiff of clean clothes and nearly tripped over the blond dog scooting between his legs. Gripping the basket tightly, he used the doorframe to regain his balance when Miki came up behind him.

"You okay?" The singer swung the door open the rest of the way, then clicked his tongue at the dog. "I don't know what the hell is going on with him. You know him. He's not that much of an asshole."

"Probably because he hasn't really been up here, so everything is new." Forest sniffed, catching a brief odor he couldn't identify. "Do you smell that?"

The room at the end of the hall was a bit difficult for Forest and Connor to furnish after they began the process of fostering Tate. Connor fought with his desire to fill the room with everything he thought a little boy would want, and Forest hated being the voice of reason, putting the brakes on quite a few outlandish ideas. A large bed was necessary, mostly so there would be space for Tate to grow into. Sticking to clean lines and neutral colors, the dresser and nightstands would match any bedding or curtains, but the industrial-style desk set up against the windows and quirky lamps gave the space character. There were bookshelves on the long wall across from the back windows, and over the past few weeks, they'd been filled up with a few novels and some boxed science experiments.

As empty as the room felt when Tate arrived, it slowly gained small hints of the boy's personality. The external monitor plugged into his school laptop flashed through pieces of artwork he'd done, as well as photos taken during the time he'd been there. The wall to the left of his desk now held posters he and Forest found during a stroll through a festival market. Without a doubt, Tate enjoyed color, sometimes losing himself to the point of deafness when illustrating in one of his sketchbooks. Some of the markers they'd grabbed at an art store were pungent, but the smell lingering in Forest's nose was more sulfur than chemical ink.

"I don't smell—" Miki sniffed once, and then Dude elbow-crawled out from under Tate's bed, a cracked-open butter container clenched in his teeth, and the stench following the dog filled the room. "What the fuck do you have?"

Gagging, Miki coughed uncontrollably but grabbed at the blond terrier attempting to escape through the open door. Dude scooted to the left, taking Miki out of the game with a quick shift of direction. Caught up in his game of take-away with Miki, the dog didn't see Forest behind him until it was too late.

"Gotcha," Forest grunted as he snatched the dog up. Squirming, Dude jerked his head around, and gravity grabbed a hold of the container's contents, tumbling the sludgy mess toward the floor.

Instinct probably drove Miki to react as quickly as he did, or so Forest figured. It went against all reason for the lean singer to grab at the tub's contents, but when the mound of rotted brussels sprouts and hot dog slivers slushed out, Miki's hand was right there to catch it.

"WE'RE HOME!" Connor called out from the foyer. Spotting Forest through the wide-framed opening to the living room, he gave his husband a quick sympathetic smile as he jerked his head toward the closet space under the stairwell. "Tate, go over and sit down with Forest. We've got something we want to talk to you about."

The boy stalled, frozen in a bent-over position as he was taking off his sneakers. There was a flash of terror across his face; then his expression dulled, forming a hard mask. Straightening up, Tate lifted his chin and squared his shoulders. "What did I do wrong?"

There were so many conflicting emotions the boy thought he was hiding, but they crept out of the tremble in his young voice. It broke Connor's heart to hear the injured defiance lingering beneath Tate's tired resignation. He knew taking the boy in would be difficult—not so much for Tate but for himself. His experience growing up in the Morgan household did not prepare him for the reality of raising a child from the streets. As grateful as he was for Forest's guidance, Connor was shattered when he learned his husband's past and the environment he grew up in was a filthy mess of neglect and degradation.

When he broached the subject with Forest, trying to feel out the edges of a conversation he didn't know how to start, Forest replied, "Shit, at least I didn't have it as bad as Miki."

The casual dismissal of the life-threatening struggles Forest faced as a child confused Connor as much as the stark realization that Miki—Kane's mercurial husband—was somehow the highest scorer in a game nobody wanted to win.

"You're not in trouble," Connor reassured the boy as he unhooked his equipment belt from his hips. "Let me just put my gear up and I'll join you guys in there."

After punching in the code for the closet door, Connor quickly separated his ammo from his weapons, then opened the standing gun safe he'd cemented into the Victorian's foundation. A practiced sweep of the safe's contents confirmed his other weapons were accounted for. Then he slid everything he'd been carrying into their places on the shelves. Slinging his equipment belt onto its hook in the closet, he could hear Forest attempting to draw Tate into casual conversation, but it did not sound as if the boy was cooperating. A few guttural replies floated down the hall, and Connor grimaced as he locked down his equipment closet.

The light storm teasing at the city's hilly neighborhoods deepened its flirtation, sliding a milky dove film over the skies. Sitting a few feet from the street, the Victorian's main window looked out onto the stand of trees lining the sidewalk. Sporadic gusts of wind whipped at the leaves; then a roll of thunder shook the air.

Coming through the smaller entry at the far side of the living room, Connor once again felt the now familiar sensation of drowning in a murky pool of uncertainty and doubt. His heavy boots weighed down each step, and he was grateful to reach the love seats bracketing the couch where Forest and Tate sat.

Despite dreading what he was going to wade into, Connor acknowledged the irony of his situation. He had a knack for planning tactical strikes on both residential and commercial raids, proud of the high result numbers up on the performance boards. His team not only enjoyed working with each other but also with him, growing as a unit while gaining experience with every new encounter. Yet here he was, trying to decide which love seat to sit on. Choosing the one next to Forest would present a united front but also would be a wall of authority Tate might feel he had to challenge. Choosing to sit next to the boy presented its own problems. He would feel trapped and forced to bounce his attention back and forth between two adults he didn't fully trust yet.

He sat down next to Forest, then began to casually unlace his boots, hoping the familiar routine of seeing Connor coming home from work would ease some of the boy's tension.

"You're not in trouble, Tate." Barefoot with one leg pulled up and tucked into the corner of the couch, Forest appeared loose and relaxed.

His kind dark eyes were slightly troubled, but the corners of his mouth were lifted into a half smile. At some point in the day, he must have been sitting like that before with a pen or marker in his hand, because his big toe boasted several thin blue squiggles near its nail.

"Then why are you going to yell at me?" The boy sat in a tense knot, his hands gripping the seat cushion. "Did I do something at school?"

"First off, we're not going to yell at you." As much as he and Forest had discussed the situation on the phone, there was really no good starting point Connor could find to land on. Taking a deep breath, he plunged in. "And school is fine, but that's not what we wanted to talk to about."

Thankfully, Forest either picked up on Connor's desperate, silent plea for help or, more than likely, a much better understanding of what Tate needed to hear.

"I want you to know that no one is mad at you, okay?" Forest waited until Tate gave a small nod. "Great. Don't forget that, okay? And something did happen today when I was putting your clothes away in your room. Miki came over so we could work on some music, and he brought Dude with him."

"I missed Dude?" Tate scowled slightly. "That sucks."

"They'll be coming over this weekend, so don't worry." Connor chuckled. "If not sooner."

"Thing is, Dude followed me upstairs, and you know how we always tell you to make sure not to leave food where he can get at it?" Tate nodded again, and Forest gently continued, his baritone soft and soothing. "Dude has a very good sense of smell, and he kind of found the food containers you had under your bed."

It was hard to watch Tate's face lose color and panic take him over. With everything they'd discussed over the phone, Forest had cautioned Connor about how Tate would react. And sadly, the drummer's predictions were right.

Stumbling off the couch, Tate tried to bolt for the door, but Connor was there to catch him. Scooping the boy up, he stood still and held him, taking the brunt of his furious, terrified blows as Tate fought to get free. The animalistic sounds coming from the boy were interspersed with stomach-clenching sobs, his legs flailing against Connor's thighs while he beat at Connor's shoulders and head. Forest was halfway off the couch when Connor shook his head, reassuring his husband he had everything under control.

The panicked onslaught lasted for what seemed like an eternity, but eventually the boy's adrenaline-fueled energy wore down, leaving him limp and weeping. Tate felt so fragile in Connor's arms, and he cradled the boy against him, working his way back to the couch. When Forest reached for Tate, his tender touch summoned up another wave of tears, but neither one of them let go. Keeping the boy between them, they sat on the couch and waited, sometimes murmuring soft assurances while the rain lashed at the bay windows.

Eventually the tears subsided and Tate was left with a breathless shudder, his eyes swollen and red and his lower lip split where he bit it. Connor realized he was gently rocking Tate and laughed when Forest asked them if they could lean toward the other side of the couch because his foot was stuck under them and they were heavy.

Staring at the floor, Tate mumbled, "Are you going to give me back?"

"I told you, kiddo, we are going to fight to keep you for as long as you want to be here." Making a playful face at Tate, Connor was gladdened to hear him suppress a giggle. "But that doesn't mean we aren't going to have to make adjustments along the way. You understand that, right? That as we figure things out, rules and other stuff might change so they work better. Here, sit down on the couch between us and let's talk this out."

When Forest told him about Tate squirreling away food underneath his bed, Connor was both hurt and confused. He'd thought Tate was happy, secure in knowing that he would be cared for. It felt both like a slap in the face and abject failure. Forest listened silently as Connor vented and growled around his feelings, then cut through the Gordian knot of conflicting emotions with a single concise argument sharpened with bare truth.

"This isn't about you," Forest replied. "It's not about us. It's about always being let down by the people that are supposed to take care of you. I'm glad that you don't understand. I can't tell you how fucking happy I am about that. And this isn't a contest about who had it better or worse.

"It's about…. It's kind of like everybody else grows up with their feet on the ground, but some of us grow up on top of a gallows with a rope around our necks. The floor feels really solid, but there is a trap door somewhere in the boards, and sometimes we've fallen through it.

"The worst part is, you end up choking and scared, sure that you're going to die because you know nobody's going to pull you up. Some people don't make it. They can't reach the rope and climb back up or they're too tired. It isn't that he doesn't trust us or have faith in us, Con, it's just that he can't afford to. Because no one's ever pulled him up and taken off that rope."

Sitting on the couch with his husband and the little boy they'd taken in, Connor realized how much he owed Brigid and Donal. He'd never doubted his parents loved him. That was a given in the Morgan household. There were arguments—sometimes to the point of furious wars—as well as mistakes made and forgiven, not only by the Morgan brood but also by their parents. He'd grown up knowing what it was like to hear he was loved and received apologies from both his father and mother when they'd been in the wrong.

Having Brigid and Donal embrace Forest as their own meant more than Connor realized, especially since he was now going to have to rise to the challenge of raising Tate to accept the same kind of love his parents gave his family.

"I didn't know how to get rid of it without you guys finding out," Tate confessed. "It was really bad smelling, and I didn't know what to do."

"Well, I cleaned everything out because I didn't want you to have to do that, okay? It was icky, but Miki helped, mostly by making sure Dude didn't get in the way." Forest bent forward, drawing closer to Tate. "I understand why you brought stuff up to keep. I get it. When I was a kid, sometimes it was hard to get food, so I would take things and hide them in my backpack or the sleeping bag I had. Thing is, I usually would eat it—or some of it—over the next few days because I was hungry."

"Hopefully, if you're ever feeling hungry," Connor interjected. "You know you can just go to the kitchen and get something to eat, right?"

Tate nodded, breaking eye contact with Connor to stare at the floor again. "I don't know why, but I just get scared."

"I still get scared sometimes too." Forest wrinkled his nose. "Now that I have the money to buy things, it's hard not to just get everything I like. I have to remember that I don't need to, mostly because it'll get stale before it gets eaten so I'm just wasting money. But, how about if we do something together until you feel like you're okay with everything?

"I've got a bin in the pantry. It's all empty, but I think what we can do after dinner is maybe fill it with some food you like that's going to last. Not to eat but to keep. If you're hungry, we still want you to go to the kitchen and grab food." Forest smiled when Connor reached over to rub his shoulder. "There's ramen and some canned SpaghettiOs. Anything that's airtight and the bugs can't get to it."

"Or the dog," Tate muttered.

"Especially the dog," Connor laughed, relieved to see the tension beginning to drain away from Tate's stiff body. "Now, in the spirit of no one being in trouble, how about if we have some pizza delivered and watch a movie? And you can even pick the toppings, T. Just no anchovies."

The boy shot him a quizzical look. "What are those?"

"Fish, kiddo. Little salty dead-eyed fish." Connor mimicked Tate's disgusted look. "Hey, it's not my thing. Miki likes them. Even on pizza. But I promise, I'll raise you better than that. And if you agree to some vegetables, I might even let you pick the movie."

CHAPTER NINE

"YOU SURE you're okay with picking them up? Because Marcy's mom said she would be happy to swing by."

Connor loved his husband. It wasn't something he forgot, but sometimes he needed to repeatedly mutter it under his breath, especially while having the same conversation over the phone for five minutes while he maneuvered through afternoon traffic. It had been easy enough to shake loose from work after Forest texted him, asking if it would be at all possible to grab Tate and the other kids who made up the Friday carpool. It was normally something Brigid did, using the car drives to not only bond with their foster son but also to spoil the hell out of him. It took nearly an act of God to get her to stop buying the kids ice cream on the way home, and there were still times when he and Forest received texts from Brigid and Donal informing them that Tate would either be attending a ballgame that afternoon or spending the night at the Morgans' family home.

Connor wasn't sure who the woman was that picked his boy up every Friday, but he was pretty certain it wasn't the same Irish firebrand who told him he couldn't go out to play until he got all of his homework done.

"I am three minutes out at the most." Connor forced himself to lighten his tone, knowing that even a hint of growl in his voice would stroke Forest the wrong way. "Actually, I'm even closer than that. I can see the end of the pickup line for the school."

His husband was already on edge, torn between obligations to his band and seeing to the needs of his family. There was already a press of guilt on Forest for not being there for Tate even as Connor assured him things were fine. He never would've imagined that his fairly low-key drummer would turn into a high-strung worrier, but having Tate in their lives seemed to have triggered something deep in Forest's psyche.

"I wish I could have given them a heads-up that you are the one grabbing them today."

"Well next time, I'll tell my mum to sprain her ankle in the morning." From the guttural swearing coming over the line, Connor got the feeling Forest was in no mood to be teased. "*A ghra*, I've got this. Once I get up to the curb and park, I'll get out so he can see me. And it's not like he doesn't know what I drive. It'll be fine."

There was more indistinct muttering, and then Forest said, "Just watch out for some of those soccer moms. They can get a little vicious."

"Have you met who raised me?" Connor let a small import car into the line ahead of him, lifting his hand to acknowledge the *thank-you* honk the driver gave him once she was fully in the lane. "Go back to the guys, and I'll take care of our kid. Just let me know later if you guys are going to pull an all-nighter. That way I don't wait up and worry you ended up in a ditch driving home."

"We live in San Francisco. Where the hell are you finding ditches?" There was a heavy sigh, then Forest said, "You're going to have to get out anyway and check in with the teacher on duty. I know you're on all of the kids' pickup lists, but not everyone there knows you. Tate's the only one who needs a booster seat, but don't let Peter talk you into letting him sit in the front seat. They all go in the back."

"Got it." The line moved a few car lengths forward, then came to a complete stop again. He was close enough to be able to see the front of the school, and from the harried gesturing of a woman holding a clipboard near the building's entrance, Connor assumed that was the teacher he would have to check in with. "How do the other parents deal with the booster seat issue if their kids don't need it?"

"Everyone still had one. The others just hit eight before Tate did, and he'll be out of it soon, remember? His birthday is coming up."

"Speaking of birthdays, Mum wants to throw the kid a huge party." An entire crowd of identical-looking children swarmed around the clipboard-wielding teacher and began to fling themselves through the open doors of a maroon Toyota a few lengths ahead of Connor's SUV. "And there is some poor parent in front of me doing a reverse clown car act. They must have packed fifteen kids into that Sienna."

"That's probably what your mom's car looked like when she had to pick up her horde." Forest's voice was muffled for a moment, but Connor could hear him tell someone it would be a few more minutes before he came back. "And as for a party, how about if we ask Tate what he wants to do?"

"Think he'd be honest?" It was a valid question, especially given Tate's reluctance to speak up about things he liked or wanted. "I know his therapist said we need to reassure him we're going to try to make sure he's not going anywhere, but it seems like the longer he's with us, the more scared he is that someone from CPS is going to take him away. I asked him if he wanted to get those Converses he saw the other day, and he told me he probably wouldn't have room for them in his backpack."

"We just have to keep hammering away at it," his husband replied. "I'd like to tell you that goes away, but it kind of doesn't. It's hard to get over. How about if we talk to him tomorrow morning over some waffles and come up with a plan we can give your mom? Because it's not like she's going to let us plan anything ourselves."

"If you told her you wanted to plan it, she would be totally hands-off." Connor *tsk*ed playfully. "I see through the two of you. Sitting together, cackling over things, and plotting. She's finally got a kid who loves holidays and celebrations like she does. Just whatever the two of you decide to do, no ponies. Okay?"

"Like don't buy him a pony, or we just can't have ponies at the party?" Forest laughed at Connor's groan. "I'm going to get back to it before Damie beats me over the head with something. I'll call you later and let you know how things are. Oh shit, you came from work. I don't know how they're going to be about your gun."

"Already locked down in the back. Just wearing my technical uniform, got my star and my winning personality." If ever Connor heard someone roll their eyes, he was pretty certain Forest was doing just that. "If I can storm through a drug raid, I'm pretty sure I can handle a kid pickup. Stop worrying."

"Love you." Forest huffed out a chuckle. "And since I'm pretty sure you are your mother's son, when you stop for ice cream, don't let Pete get anything with strawberries. It's not going to kill him, but he's kind of allergic."

"Got it. No strawberries, and I love you too. Tell whoever is going to be the adult over there tonight, make sure they get some food into you guys." Now stuffed to the gills with children, the Toyota eased away from the curb and the line began to move again. "Talk to you later, babe. It's my turn to retrieve the spawn."

SCHOOLS WERE quite different from when Connor and his pack ran amok through the hallowed halls of the Catholic institution his parents enrolled their children in. The wood-and-glass buildings were spaced out around large swatches of fragrant grass, and enormous spreading trees sheltered the worn-down paths through the school's front lawn. A broad overhang stretched along the length of the main structure, its double doors propped open, allowing students to roam in and out. A beefy-armed woman dressed in a school-colored T-shirt and shorts manned the entrance, a bright metal whistle dangling from a lanyard around her neck. A few feet down the sidewalk, the curly-haired woman Connor had spotted earlier stopped each child as they came forward. She listened briefly to what they had to say, then checked something off on the pages pinned to her clipboard. Dismissing each child with a quick smile, she waited for the students to climb into the waiting cars and began motioning for a line to move.

As much as Connor liked his old H2, it had been past time to put the old workhorse to pasture. Handing its keys over to his baby brother Riley was almost a rite of passage among the Morgan children. Cars, like clothes and furniture, were often handed down, and in the case of the H2, any bickering between Riley and his twin, Kiki, was headed off when Kane went car shopping with Connor and came home with his own new SUV. The Defender was easily modified to serve as a utility vehicle for Connor's work, but he'd been surprised at how smooth it drove, especially through tight traffic. With the other cars cleared away, Connor discovered he was the first in line, so he moved the SUV as far forward as he could, easing the nose of the vehicle close to the beginning of the fire lane. Then he stepped out of the car, turned on the alarm, walked around to the sidewalk, and spotted a private security guard hustling toward him.

The man was older, probably in his late fifties, and he moved with purpose toward Connor. His approach was steady but with a calm authority. Nodding a greeting, he wiped at the thick ginger mustache nearly covering his upper lip.

"What can I do for you—" The older man's sharp blue eyes flicked toward the star and name tag fixed to Connor's SWAT uniform. "Lieutenant? Is there a problem?"

Nodding his head toward the teacher at the end of the walk, Connor said, "I'm doing a pickup for my kid and his carpool. First time, so I've got to do the whole song and dance so they'll let me take the monsters home."

"Let me introduce you to Miss Mary," the guard replied. "Just watch her or you'll be volunteering for the bake sales every first Sunday. That's how I picked up these five pounds around my belly that I can't get rid of."

Connor was within six feet of the teacher when he heard Tate shout his name. Bursting through the open door, the boy ran down the sidewalk, his backpack gripped in one hand and nearly dragging alongside him. A pair of children Connor recognized from periodic visits trailed behind Tate, their longer legs quickly catching up with him. With one hand nearly trapped in his back pocket while retrieving his wallet, Connor was almost knocked over when Tate skidded into him. The other children avoided the collision, but Peter somehow got his leg tangled in his own backpack and almost fell face first before Marcy made a quick grab for his arm.

"Hi, Mr. Morgan." With what looked like a practiced swerve, Marcy righted the lanky towheaded boy and pulled him to his feet. Pete mumbled something Connor couldn't make out, then wiped his nose. "Hold on, I've got a tissue."

"I didn't know you were picking us up!" Tate's exuberance faded into a worried frown. "Is Birdie okay?"

"She's fine, kiddo." Connor moved his free arm around Tate, giving him a quick squeeze. "She tweaked her ankle, so I came instead. Let me go show my ID to Miss Mary or she's not going to let you guys come home with me and I'll have to call someone higher up the food chain to grab you."

There were a few other children and a couple of women clustered around the teacher as Connor approached. He met her warm gaze over the heads of four little girls chattering away about a movie they were going to see over the weekend. While she checked their names on the list, the two women standing nearby both smiled at Connor, and the blonder of the two sidled over, holding her hand out when she got to Connor's side.

"Hello. I don't think I've ever seen you do a pickup before." Her voice was husky and low, but the grip she had on Connor's hand held firmly when he tried to draw it back. "I'm sure I would've recognized your... car... if I'd seen it."

"Yes, definitely the first time." Regaining possession of his hand, Connor peeked around the blond, hoping the check-in teacher was finally free. "My husband or my mother usually grabs the kids. Excuse me, let me catch the teacher before she gets tied up with somebody else."

Verifying his identity and approval for the carpool was quick, just not as fast as the warning about the barracuda on the sidewalk Miss Mary gave him before he stepped away. Connor was still laughing as he gathered up the three kids and got them settled into the Defender.

"I hate sitting in this chair thing," Tate complained as he fastened the seat belt around his waist. "It makes me feel like a baby."

"You don't have much longer to go, kid," Connor reminded him as he climbed into the driver's seat. "Now, I was told by a certain Birdie about a Friday ritual called ice cream cone. Anyone back there interested?"

"ARE YOU sure you know what you're doing?" Tate's skepticism was as thick as the block of cheddar cheese Connor was grating into a glass bowl. "Forest always uses white cheese."

"We don't have any. It'll be fine," he reassured the despotic sous chef he'd asked to help him. So far, Tate had only offered opinions about what Connor was doing wrong, but if he were honest with himself, he remembered having a lot of his own thoughts about his mother's cooking certain things. "Sometimes Mexican lasagna can have different things in it. This time it's going to be cheddar cheese instead of cotija. Trust me, we're not going to die from it."

"Marcy says Mexican lasagna isn't a real thing." Reaching over toward the bowl, Tate grabbed a quick pinch of cheese, then stuffed it in his mouth.

"Well, considering some of her family comes from Mexico, I would say we could trust her judgment on that." Tapping the grater free of any cheese shreds clinging to its insides, Connor mentally measured if he had enough for the casserole. "It's something my mum made us when we were kids, and it isn't even some of the crazier stuff she fed us. I think it's kind of like Hawaiian pizza. Nothing about that is Hawaiian, but that's how it was sold to people so that's the name that stuck. Pretty sure a real Hawaiian pizza would have kalua pig and cooked taro leaves on it. You know, nothing says we can't change the name."

For an almost eight-year-old little boy, Tate seemed to have cornered the market on giving dubious looks. "It's written that way in the recipe book. We can't change it."

"If something is wrong and we know that, we should always push to change it," Connor replied.

It was strange to hear his father's words fall out of his own mouth. It felt surreal to relive a moment as the other side of the discussion but Connor also knew what thought-gerbils Tate had running around in his brain. Having your world shoved open by possibilities always took a moment or two to process, and from the scowl on his son's face, Connor imagined those gerbils were working overtime.

"We can always put white-out tape over the title and write in a better one on top of it." After wiping his hands on a dish towel, Connor leaned on the island. "What would you call it?"

"We shouldn't call it Mexican, right?"

"I would agree that it's not very authentic. It has those kinds of flavors in it, but I wouldn't call it Mexican."

The spiral-bound book was something his mother gave them after their wedding—a thick volume of cut-out recipes and old favorites copied and pasted into a software program then printed out. There were notes in the columns of practically every recipe Brigid included in the book, her swooping cursive sharing a story about the food or which family member considered it a favorite. Connor couldn't find a date for the casserole they were making, but he was fairly certain it was from the midsixties or early seventies, something found in a school community cookbook sold by the students to fund a field trip or something equally expensive.

In the weeks since they'd taken him home, Tate's personality had slowly crept out from behind the stoic mask he showed the world. Practically deadly serious, his humor was droll and dry, but his curiosity was endless. Sometimes his questions flew out of him in rapid-fire bursts, while other times, he had thoughtful pauses before he asked someone to elaborate or clarify their point. Fear no longer dominated his movements, but there was still a healthy dose of suspicion in his expressions and mannerisms. Trust was a continuing issue, but he and Forest discovered giving Tate some say or influence over certain things helped strengthen the connection between them. Right now, asking Tate to alter something as simple as a recipe title might have seemed frivolous to a lot of people, but the boy definitely was ready to tackle it as if it were his sacred duty.

"It's got a lot of the same stuff as tacos," Tate pointed out, running his finger over the recipe page. "Maybe instead of Mexican lasagna we call it taco lasagna?"

"I am definitely on board with that. Taco lasagna it is," he agreed, then jerked his chin up toward the cookbook. "Now do your job and tell me how much diced onion I need."

Tate studied the recipe, then pronounced, "*Amháin cupán.*"

"*Maith. Dún.*" Connor praised the boy. "But you have to reverse the words. It's *cupán amháin.* Cup comes first. But you said it right. Good job."

Despite the darkening sky outside, a burst of sunlight broke across the kitchen in Tate's broad grin. Leaning forward on his elbows, he rested against the island's rounded edge, wiggling a bit in his seat. Working the skin off a sweet Maui onion, Connor glanced at the upside-down writing on the page sitting between them, double-checking the amount just to be sure.

"Did you have fun this afternoon with Marcy and Pete?" In the hour he had all three children, Connor was amazed at the ruckus they threw.

Plastic dinosaurs and toy fighter jets were used in an epic battle, although Connor wasn't quite sure about who the good guys were or even if the kids cared. Somehow along the way, the thunderous lizards became mounts for space cowboys and a galaxy-wide revolution was born. As if they coordinated the timing, both Marcy and Pete's mothers arrived within seconds of each other, looking a lot more well rested than Connor felt. It was only after he'd packed up the other two children and cleared the living room battlefield that he realized he was still wearing his uniform.

"It was really cool," Tate piped up. "I think Marcy's mom likes you. She kept looking at your butt."

The offhand comment momentarily stunned Connor, and he glanced up at the boy. There was so much to say that he couldn't find the beginning of his thoughts. Grabbing at a lingering tail of something mostly solid, he finally replied, "I don't think she was looking at my butt. She was probably trying to figure out why I was still dressed for work."

"No, it was definitely your butt." Tate gave a snort Connor was fairly certain he'd stolen off Miki. "Marcy said if you weren't married to Forest, her mom would probably hit on you. I told her it wouldn't matter because you don't like girls."

"Well, I do like girls, but I like Forest better." Connor finished chopping the onions, then realized he didn't have anything to put them in. As important as *mise en place* was to the cooking process, his goal was to do as few dishes as possible, so he dumped the cubes into the same bowl he put his minced garlic in. "Next?"

"One large can of black olives, sliced." Tate glanced at the can. "I don't think those are sliced."

"They're not, but I can chop them roughly so they're about the same size as the onions." The can hissed when Connor popped the top open, splashing brine over the counter. "Slicing them would be a pain. My fingers are too big to hold them steady. I'd probably end up cutting myself."

Tate grunted as if acknowledging Connor's hands were too large. Bringing his own hands up, the boy studied them intently. His frame was delicate and lithe and his facial features were sculpted more by his Asian genetics than anything else. As much as Tate resembled Miki St. John, his mannerisms were becoming more and more like Forest, an amicable and curious soul focused on exploring the world around him.

His expressions were also easier to read because Connor quickly spotted the moment Tate's brain churned out a question.

Tilting his head, Tate asked, "So if you like girls, why did you marry Forest?"

"That is a very good question," Connor acknowledged with a nod while he hacked at a few olives on the chopping board. "It's because I fell in love with him. And sometimes love—your heart and soul—finds your person when you least expect it. It took me a while to understand how I felt about Forest, and that wasn't a bad thing. I knew I liked him, and he made me feel things inside of myself that no one else ever had. So while I knew I always liked girls, I also realized that I liked some guys as well. But I really loved Forest, and the thought of him not being in my life made me really sad."

"Is that how Birdie feels about Donal?" Tate nibbled on an olive he stole from the open can.

"Yes, I think they feel that way about each other." Another batch of minced olives were added to the growing mound on the chopping board. "I grew up knowing they loved me, and I saw how they are with each other. So when I met Forest, I kind of understood what I was feeling because I knew what that kind of love looked like. Does that make sense to you?"

"Yeah, I think so." The wheels spun again and another question percolated up to the surface. "Do you think Birdie loves me?"

The longing in Tate's voice nearly broke Connor's heart. Setting the knife down, he reached for a clean tea towel, then wiped his hands. A few steps took him around the island, and he stopped himself just short of touching distance from the boy. He'd moved too quickly, triggering Tate's semi-wild nature. The boy's eyes grew wide, startled to the point where he half slid off the chair, his bare toes touching the kitchen floor. His limbs were rigid, and he trembled, poised in midflight, trapped in the confusion of his need to be comforted and the instinct to flee to keep himself safe.

Connor crouched, resting his weight on his left knee. Every part of him screamed to grab Tate into a fierce hug, but a rational part of his mind whispered to go slower, to ask permission, and more importantly, to let the frightened boy who still wore bruises on his soul decide what he needed.

"Sorry, kiddo." Grimacing apologetically, Connor gave Tate a small shrug. "I just wanted to give you a hug and—"

Tate's arms were around Connor's neck before he could finish speaking. After wrapping his arms around the slender boy, Connor reached up to cup the back of Tate's head, cradling him closer. Eventually, the boy's body stopped trembling.

"I know Brigid—Birdie—loves you. So does Donal and Forest and everyone else, including me." There was a space inside of Connor's heart that hadn't been there before, or more than likely, he hadn't noticed it growing deep within him.

Holding Tate until his fear bled out touched off something fierce in Connor. He had no name for the swelling emotion, but he recognized it, having seen it in his parents' eyes, heard it in their voices when they rose up to defend him and others. The intensity of what flooded through Connor's soul scared him to the marrow of his bones. He would die for the little boy he held. And he would kill for him too.

"We don't finish up this taco lasagna, we are going to starve tonight. And it's not like we can have ice cream for dinner, because we already had some this afternoon," Connor whispered into Tate's ear as he rocked back and forth. "But I want you to remember, we all love you, and we want the best for you. Forest and I are going to do everything in our power to make sure you are safe. Okay?"

"Okay," Tate squeaked. "You gotta let go. I can't breathe."

"Sorry, kiddo. Here, catch some air." Connor gently eased the boy back and straightened Tate's rumpled shirt. "You know what I realized? The recipe calls for green chiles, and I don't think we have any. Do we just want to use pico de gallo?"

"That's not spicy." The disgusted look he got back from Tate was nearly as strong as the hug Connor gave him. "I think I have a can of chipotle in my bin. I can go get it."

Connor contemplated for a second, then replied, "We can do an exchange. I use the chipotle and you can grab something out of the pantry to take its place."

"Nah, it's all good. It'll be my part of the dinner." Tate stepped away, then turned back to Connor and said, "And I love Birdie and the rest of you guys too."

"I know, kiddo." Connor ruffled Tate's hair, then stood up, stretching back to loosen a tightness in his thighs. "And you know what I'm going to do while you grab that can? I'll give a ring over to Birdie and Donal to see if they want to eat dinner with us. Because I bet you they'll not only say yes, but they'll bring something over for dessert."

CHAPTER
TEN

IT WAS unlikely the weather would cooperate and be clear on a Saturday afternoon, yet following a swirl of pea soup fog in the morning, some benevolent God set the sun on high to burn away the gloom. And if the suddenly clear day hadn't left Forest slightly speechless, the nearly military precison of the Morgan family setting up their backyard for Tate's birthday party stole any words he might have had left.

Before they left the Victorian, his small family had a ceremonial celebration around the removal of Tate's booster seat from the back of both their vehicles. Following an intense battle where Connor and Tate advocated they complete the ritual with a bonfire to dispose of the boosters, Forest resoundingly beat down the request, reminding both of the stubborn males not only of the cost of the seats but of how they would benefit another family who couldn't afford something new. Rather than acquiescing to common sense, the pair amped up their argument, only for Forest to not only shoot it down again, but as a consequence for advocating the eventual destruction of perfectly good seats they could donate, Forest made them scrub the boosters down, dry them off, and then repack them in their original boxes they'd saved in the garage's attic storage.

Fortified with a waffle-and-bacon brunch at one of Connor's favorite diners, they'd headed over to the Morgan family home where Forest once again realized how useless he was when confronted with Brigid's army of offspring. He made a few attempts but only got in the way, and after Donal stepped on him twice, Forest was led to one of the comfortable padded patio chairs, given a tumbler of iced coffee, and told to sit there and be pretty while they got things done.

His protests were met with patronizing nods. Then, not more than a minute later, Miki was sent to join him, carrying his own coffee after being kissed by a distracted Kane. The second oldest Morgan seemed to know exactly what was needed among his pack of siblings, because he trotted over to the canopy construction area and began to unfold several long tables lying on the ground nearby.

"You didn't bring Dude?" Forest peered around the cluttered backyard, trying to spot the blond terrier potentially hiding among the pieces of pop-up canopies the Morgans were assembling a few yards from the pool.

"He got as far as the kitchen, then told me to fuck off. There's food and the kid in there." Easing carefully down onto the lounger, Miki gingerly lifted his leg up and over to rest on the chair. "I got kicked out before I even said hello to anyone."

"You okay?" Forest sat up, worried for the singer. Despite having several surgeries, the knee injury Miki sustained during the accident that killed half of his first band's members still troubled him at times. "Do you want me to go in and grab you some ibuprofen or something?"

"Nah, I'm okay. Thanks, though. I took some before we left." Miki groaned as he rubbed his knee. "I think I just overstretched it. Sometimes you end up doing things thinking it'll be okay, but when it's all done, it is *so* not okay. You'd think I'd know better. Especially after Kane's pulled long hours on a case."

"What did you do?" While Miki often took Dude on rambles in their Chinatown neighborhood, he was pretty good about knowing his limits, and Forest couldn't imagine him going on a long walk during the rains they'd been having. "Did one of the doctors give you a new physical therapy thing to do? That thing with the bands and lifting up your feet is already crazy. Just that one time and it felt like my calves were on fire every time I bent over."

"Are you serious right now?" Miki stopped his rubbing and glanced over at Forest.

Stymied, Forest stared back at his friend. "What? They're always giving you new stuff to do with your knee."

"Man, Kane said we should take the Tater for a weekend to give you guys some alone time, and I told him he was nuts. Maybe not."

"I don't understand." Forest briefly flirted with the idea of Tate spending a weekend with Kane and Miki. "You want to borrow the kid?"

In a lot of ways it was a ludicrous suggestion. Being one of the older Morgans, Kane had a lot of experience with kids, while Miki was more inclined to let Tate run wild. The singer's feral nature left him with few boundaries and a skewed common sense. Still, it was a tempting idea, especially since it would allow Tate unfettered access to his favorite soul in the world—Miki's terrier, Dude.

"Okay. Think about it." Shaking his head, Miki stretched out his legs, seemingly working out a few kinks. "Kane has the day off after working round the clock for the past couple of weeks on his murder case. The band doesn't have practice scheduled. And the two of us don't need to be anywhere until the afternoon for your kid's party. Look over at Connor and tell me the first thing that pops into your head."

At some point in the party organization, Connor had stripped off his hoodie and tossed it onto an empty chair. His tank top strained with the stretch of his thickly muscled shoulders and back as he helped Kane anchor canopy legs with sand-filled weight bags. The brothers were laughing over something, nearly identical off-kilter smiles pushing dimples into their cheeks. Connor's biceps bulged when he grasped a bag Kane passed over to him, but he swung it easily around the pole, then strapped the weight's Velcro ties together to hold it in place.

They were both handsome, vibrant men with a firm grasp of their place in the world, but Forest's heart only skipped with deep need when his gaze settled on Connor.

He knew the taste of Connor's mouth. His skin remembered the touch of his husband's callused hands and the sharp bite of Con's teeth. There wasn't an inch on his body that didn't know the Irish cop's kiss, and his arms knew the shape of Connor's body against them. He'd lost sleep waiting for Connor to return after a long night of fighting back the darkness eating away at the edges of the city they loved and didn't regret one minute they spent wrapped around each other when Con finally came through the door.

What Miki meant finally sank in, and Forest muttered, "Oh! *Fuck.*"

"Yeah. *That.*" Miki laughed. "I swear to God, sometimes talking to you is like explaining venison jerky to Bambi."

The family could forget about using a barbecue for the frankfurters later on, because Forest was pretty sure his face was red and hot enough to put a good char on them. He didn't know what was more embarrassing, having Miki explain to him about what he meant or that any random discussion of sex always brought a flush to his face.

"This is so stupid. I'm in a damned rock band. I can talk about sex." He touched his iced coffee to his cheek. "I shared a van, hotel rooms, and underwear with you guys, and I can't stop fucking blushing."

"I'm more worried that it took you this long to figure it out." Miki nodded toward Kane and Connor. "Seriously, it might really be a good idea for you guys to get a day or two to yourselves. We can take him. Might have to fight—what does he call her? Birdie?—for him, but she's short. Kane could put his hand on her forehead so she can't reach to hit him, and I could sneak the kid in the car. We'd have to move and change our names, but I'd do that for you."

"There's always a lot going on," he admitted softly. "I think we are just really focused on Tate right now. I'm trying to make sure I don't screw him up. I try to be a good example. I try to show him what's right and that it's okay to feel mad or happy. But then there's always this part of me that wants to make sure he knows how to get a couple of free sodas from a vending machine or what pawnshop to go to so he can flip an EBT card to cash."

"That's because you're nice. I mean, deep down there is probably shit you haven't scraped off, and you might never be able to get to all of that." Miki slowly crossed his legs and leaned toward Forest. Golden flecks danced in his hazel eyes, but there were more folded shadows in their depths than light. "But you try to be a good person. More than try. You *are* a good person. Even if sometimes I know you want to punch someone in the face, you talk to them first. You try to understand how they got to where they are. And all of that shit you can't get off you just makes it easier to know where Tate comes from and who you are now is where he can be."

As much as Forest wanted to deny it, Miki wasn't wrong. He still struggled with the conflicting voices inside of him. His body remembered the deep fissures formed on his dry, cracked skin after a long cold winter storm and more than a few times he'd woken up hungry, only to realize it was a memory echoing some long-ago day when breakfast and lunch was ketchup soup, a stealthily made concoction from purloined condiment packages and the hot water from a tea dispenser. They moved too often for Forest to have any sense of belonging to any one place, and when he'd finally settled in as Frank's adopted distant relative, he had no sense of family, but he retained the one thing he'd nurtured for as long as he could remember.

For all the filth smeared on him, Forest was determined to be as nice a person as he could be. He'd spent so much time constantly correcting his own bad behavior, stopping to count to five before reacting, and most of all, to reach out and help even when he didn't want to.

He counted to five a lot less, especially since meeting Connor, and he couldn't remember the last time he made ketchup soup. He *liked* being nice. He liked being the rational one in the band, and he very much enjoyed having Miki as a brother.

Yet despite growing up with a mother who worked the sheets to pay her drug bill and spending quite a few nights expanding Connor's knowledge about what people could get up to in the bedroom, he still got embarrassed. Miki and Kane offering to take Tate for a weekend was a big deal and something the boy would enjoy. His uncles were two of his favorite people, even without the added bonus of Dude.

"Is this where I am supposed to say, no, I don't think we can impose on you by asking you to take Tate for a couple of days?" Forest tilted his head at his friend.

"Why the fuck would you say that? You say that kind of shit to the moms in your kid's carpool because it's like agreeing to make cupcakes to sell at a soccer game. Keep that kind of crap for the PTA where it belongs." Miki stabbed at the air toward Forest's nose. "Don't start with the fucking suburban lying just because you live in a nice house with a stupid picket fence in the front."

"I think we *have* to have a picket fence. Probably a part of the sales contract when you buy a house that old." Knowing Miki sometimes had a hard time with reading sarcasm, Forest was delighted to tease a scowl out of him. "It was either a picket fence or Connor has to start wearing sandals and white socks while mowing the lawn. Just wait. Kane's next. One morning you're going to wake up and half of your driveway is going to be all grass and he's going to be out there in Birkenstocks talking to the neighbors about gophers and crabgrass."

"Screw you," Miki shot back. "I hope some dog shits on your lawn and its owner doesn't pick it up. Not just one dog. A pack of them. Great Danes. And if I'm lucky, some asshole fed them all bean burritos and that crap hit just as they got to your house."

AFTER TWO straight hours of screaming children, endless cups of sugary foods, and two piñatas, Forest stole away to find his husband.

Even though the adults outnumbered the kids two to one, it didn't seem like enough coverage. Maybe it was the years spent playing large arenas or that all of the rest of the band members had the same chaotic energy as the alarmingly high-volume chaos of excited children, because Forest didn't think he would be the first one to break off and look for some peace and quiet. More surprisingly, Rafe and Damien were fantastic with the kids, keeping up with everything they did and, along with Braeden, making sure no one drowned in the pool. Miki hung back more, less enthusiastically engaged than the other two, but there was something about him that seemed to draw quieter ones to his side. Sitting at one of the smaller round tables, the singer listened intently to the meandering stories being told while a few of the partygoers drew pictures on large sheets of thick white butcher paper. The table became a reliable place to find calm in the thunderous storm filling the Morgans' backyard, but even in that corner of relative quiet it was too noisy for Forest, so he sought to find his own peace in the shape of the Irish cop he married.

That's when he discovered Connor was nowhere to be found.

"Try the study." Donal drawled in his thick Irish accent when Forest asked if he'd seen his oldest son. His face was warmed with years of experience, and a touch of silver glinted at his temples, but there was no mistaking where the Morgan boys got their good looks. "We've got things covered out here. Take some food with ye, and why don't ye two get something tucked in. My bride was saying something about doing the cake and gifts in about forty minutes, so if yer not out here by then, ah'll send one of the spawn to go fetch ye."

Armed with a plate of hotdogs and potato salad, Forest fought his way through the crowd to get inside. The house wasn't much quieter than the backyard, but the child count was zero, and the family room, having been declared an off-limits zone, provided a sanctuary for Dude and the Morgans' cats. The terrier looked up from his spot on the couch when Forest passed by, one suspicious eye cracked open as if to gauge how much of a threat Forest would be to his nap. Murmuring an apology to the dog, he kept walking until he reached the study door, then juggled the two plates of food so he could rap his knuckles at the frame.

"Are you under five and a half feet?" Connor's deep voice rumbled through the closed door. "If you aren't, you can come in, but make sure no one sees you."

"Open the door for me. My hands are full." Forest eased past Connor once he cracked the door open wide enough. "And your mom is under five and a half feet."

"And she's worse than the kids. I came here so my brain could breathe a little bit. She's not good for that." Connor sniffed at the air as he followed Forest to one of the leather couches placed in front of the study's fireplace. "Is that all for you, or are you going to share?"

"There's at least eight hotdogs here. If you think I can eat that much, you're crazy." After setting the food down on the coffee table, Forest flopped down onto the couch. "Shit, there's potato salad. I forgot to grab forks."

"There's some plastic ones in the drawer under the coffee machine. I'll grab some." Returning with the utensils and two cold bottles of water from the mini fridge tucked into the sideboard Donal used as a wet bar, Connor sat down and examined what Forest brought to eat. "I'm guessing the two with kimchi and mayonnaise are yours."

"You do not know what you are missing." Maneuvering one of the dogs covered with chunks of spicy pickled Napa cabbage off the plate was a little difficult, and he lost a few pieces of the kimchi along the way. "And it's not mayonnaise. It's whipped cream cheese. It just got all melty because the hotdog just came off the grill."

"That's what I get for letting you hang out with my brother's husband," Connor teased. "Next thing I know, you'll be eating anchovy-and-pineapple burritos."

"Okay, now you're just making shit up." Forest stopped before he took a bite. "It's pepperoni and pineapple *pizza*, not a burrito. Anchovies go with olives and mushrooms on a white-sauce pizza. And both of those are pretty good too. Eat your hotdogs. We've got only about half an hour before they come get us to cut the cake."

Leaning into Forest, Connor plucked up the pieces of fallen kimchi and popped them in his mouth. Chewing quickly and ignoring Forest's halfhearted protests, he fended off an attack on his potato salad with his fork when Forest attempted to stab his finger into the pale mound.

"Eat your hotdogs," Connor parroted back at Forest, then followed up with a deep kiss. "We can't miss Tate's first birthday cake."

Forest never was a fan of frankfurters growing up. His experience with them came mostly from bloated tubes of meat floating in the vats of greasy warm water found at the back of sketchy convenience stores. He ate them when offered because they were free or cheap. Corn dogs were a different matter, because the sweet bread crust around the meat was good regardless of the temperature, but naked on a stale bun was at the bottom of Forest's food lists. Oddly enough, despite his name, his foster father Frank had the same opinion about the mealy sausages as Forest did, and it wasn't until he got involved with the Morgans that Forest discovered what a good hotdog tasted like.

He also found out there were many disagreements about not only what kind of sausage tasted the best but also the proper way to cook it.

Today's offering was a family favorite, a bright red hotdog, plump and long enough to fill a standard bun with a juicy, meaty flavor hefty enough to hold up against even the spiciest of condiments. If he had a choice, it would be the only kind Forest would have in the house, but his husband had an odd affection for cheddarwurst, preferably braised in beer and served with horseradish and sauerkraut, so their freezer was stocked with both kinds, along with a bag of dinosaur-shaped chicken nuggets stashed away for movie nights.

"Kane told me Miki suggested they take the kid for a weekend," Connor said around a mouthful of hotdog.

"That's funny." The warmed cream cheese threatened to dribble off the end of the bun, so Forest licked it up before it slagged onto the carpet. "Miki told me Kane suggested it."

"Well, no matter who is lying to us, I guess they're worried we need some couple time." Putting his plate down on the table, Connor pursed his lips in thought. "He really likes both of them, and we know he loves the dog. What do you think?"

Sitting in what Forest considered one of the anchored points in the Morgans' lives, he realized he now considered the study as much of a sanctuary as any of Donal's natural children. He hadn't grown up in the sprawling butter-yellow house. There were only a few Christmases spent decorating an enormous tree whose top had to be clipped before an old wonky-winged angel could be set into its place of honor. He didn't have a million and one stories about ornaments, Easter egg hunts, fist fights with neighborhood rivals, or long summers spent running wild across Ireland's hills. His history with the Morgan clan was a short one and spotted with fraught times, but every day it grew, and every moment he spent with his husband and their family, Forest felt another thread being stitched around him, connecting him to the wondrous, chaotic fabric Connor had the sheer luck of being born into.

Staring into their future, Forest could only see a cloudy uncertainty. Bringing Tate into the fold should have been a joyous experience, but every step forward was shaky and bittersweet. It was impossible to celebrate a today when they all knew tomorrow might never be. Every unforeseen knock on the door now heralded waves of fear at the potential of finding a solemn-faced, somber government worker who would rip Tate free of the life he was having, severing the fragile, tender roots he'd set down.

Even planning the boy's birthday party was a delicate exercise in suggestions for gifts and a battle not to overwhelm him with outrageous experiences. If that knock ever came on the door, Tate couldn't roll up his life and take it with him. There was only so much space a foster child could take up, maybe a suitcase's worth if they were lucky, and anything even marginally useful would disappear because of thieving hands and mistreatment. If Tate were taken from them—*when* Tate was taken from them—he would eventually be left with nothing, probably not even remember any kind words given to him, much less retain any confidence he'd stitched together from the shreds of his self-esteem.

Leaning back, Forest said, "I think we need to push harder to adopt Tate. We need that more than a couple's weekend. Yeah, he can go spend a couple of days with them, but we've got to make sure that he comes *home* and not just the place where he lives for now. That's what I think, Con."

"Okay, then. I can do that." Connor inhaled deeply, and he held it in tight, his gaze caught somewhere in the black-and-white photos of his family spread on the walls next to the fireplace. Nodding, he released his breath and filled his fork with potato salad. "I'll get the ball rolling with CPS on Monday and see what we have to do to make it happen. Robinson being on his birth certificate is what gives them fits, but we can push there. Now, are you going to eat that last hotdog, because if you're not, pass it over so I can take care of it before we go have cake."

"That's it?" Forest canted his head to the side, edging into his husband's field of view. "No *that's a good idea* or *I love you*? Just give me the hotdog?"

Connor gave him a smoldering look that would have charred the hotdogs to a crisp if they'd been any closer. The potato salad lump on his fork joined the rest on his plate, and then Forest was caught up in a searing, breath-stealing kiss, his face cradled between Connor's large hands. He tasted of sunshine with a hint of chlorine, a splash of mustard, and the tart crisp of lime from the flavored water. Just as Forest was prepared to throw away any caution he had, Connor broke off and pulled away, but his fingers lingered along Forest's jaw.

"I love you, *a ghra*. I want everything you do. I want Tate to have our name, our family. I want to cheer him on in anything he tries, and I want to ground him for making really shitty life choices." Connor placed a tiny, gentle kiss on the corner of Forest's mouth. "And right now, I'm afraid to touch you, because if I do, we are really going to miss the rest of Tate's birthday party, and that would break all of our hearts. So how about if we pack all of this up and go outside to watch our son blow out his candles? And then later on, after we put him to bed, I can show you exactly how much I love you."

CHAPTER
ELEVEN

SUNSHINE HELD on to San Francisco's skies with a fierce bite, but the city remained relatively cool, veiled in sheets of fluffy white clouds. Despite being a Thursday afternoon, the sidewalks were filled with joggers and dogs enthusiastically leading their owners toward whatever delicious smell caught their interests. With the glorious weather came tourists, and Chinatown soon became packed with cars and crowds, vast groups of camera-wielding people flowing from one landmark to the next while others broke off to do shopping. Taking advantage of the swell of foot traffic, restaurants off the main avenues loaded up handcarts fitted with steam tables and sent them out to look for hungry tourists hoping to catch a quick bite without having to duck into a storefront. As illegal as the steam carts were, it was somewhat of an underground tradition, one steeped in bitter rivalries between hole-in-the-wall spots scrambling to make their daily expenses and the larger traditional Chinese restaurants eager to fill their tables.

In the three months since Tate's birthday party, Connor and Forest had found themselves twisted in a maze of red tape and roadblocks. The initial reach out to Ms. Stice, the department head in charge of the area's foster cases, had been a disheartening conversation about familial rights and determining whether Tate's surviving relatives would sign him over for adoption. Complicating the matter was the claim of Robinson not being Tate's father and Stice armed with a birth certificate with Robinson clearly indicated as the male parent.

"You've had the kid for months now, Con." Kane opened the rolling ice chest they'd brought to the park and extracted a couple of Diet Coke bottles. Handing one to his brother, he flipped the chest closed, then stretched his legs out in front of him. "You guys have obviously given him a better life than he had before—and I get it's to protect parental rights—but you and I both know Robinson is never going to step up for Tate."

Washington Square was close enough to Chinatown to get some breathing room from the crowds, and spread out to the shadow of the Saints Peter and Paul church, it offered a welcome quiet sanctuary despite being in the middle of a busy part of the city. After packing Connor's SUV with a few folding benches, ice chests filled with food and drink, as well as a couple of thick blankets to sit on if they needed them, Connor and Forest bundled Tate up and headed over to the park to meet Kane and Miki.

A battered Frisbee proved to be the game of choice for the musicians and the little boy, but Dude opted out of the play, flopping down at Kane's feet to enjoy the shade of the trees they'd chosen for their picnic site. The little terrier scraped one of his paws on the ice chest, staring up at Kane with his big soft brown eyes. Sighing, the younger Morgan flipped open the chest again to dig out a couple of ice cubes. After letting the lid fall back down, he plopped the ice in Dude's water dish, then shook his hand dry.

"That dog's got you as trained as his owner," Connor teased.

"Don't let Miki hear you say that." Kane cracked open the top of his soda bottle. "Dude's not his dog, remember? He just moved in and never left."

"Don't give me that bullshit. Dog's got a license and a tag." He snorted back.

"And a microchip." Taking a sip of his soda, Kane slanted a look over at Connor. "So you've got no opinion about the state and what they're doing with his adoption?"

As sturdy as the benches were, they still creaked when Connor leaned back. Scowling at the noise, he worked at releasing the bubbles from his soda bottle slowly, letting the gas seep out while each wave of foam dissipated. Forest's laughter rolled over the lawn toward them, a wave of Tate's giggles following close behind. He'd missed what happened, but from the muttered Chinese Miki flung out and the singer's long trek to retrieve the Frisbee, he gathered somebody missed.

"I have a lot of opinions." Connor dropped into Gaelic, wrapping his emotions in a language he knew could express the depth of his frustrations and dreams. "It gets harder every day. Stice assures me that no one is going to take him from us, but tell me you wouldn't fear every knock on the door or a phone call from a number you don't recognize.

"I hate not being able to make plans for his next school or dream about what college he might go to. Forest and I want him to have a connection to his mother's culture, but how do we go about that? The easiest thing would be to reach out to her family, but no one there wants to have anything to do with him." Connor reached down to scratch at the tawny dog's ears. Dude looked up and gave him a tempting smile before going back to chewing on the ice cube he'd fished out of his bowl. "What happens when he starts asking us questions about her? What do we tell him? Or worse, suppose he's taken away from us before that happens?"

Kane shook his head. "That's not going to happen."

A whiff of garlic and olive oil carried over from the Italian restaurant across the street from the park, and Connor inhaled the scent appreciatively. His stomach rumbled, reminding him the cup of coffee he had that morning was the only thing he poured down his gullet and it was past time for food. He told his belly to wait, wanting Tate to have a little bit more playtime.

Connor wanted Tate to have every single second of joy he could.

With years at the SFPD under their belt and both ranked with gold stars, he and Kane had experienced more than a few encounters with Child Protective Services, and not all of them good. Even setting aside what they knew of Miki's and Forest's past with the agency, the department didn't have a good track record. He knew in his gut Stice would do the best she could, but there was also the possibility of someone getting a wild hair up their ass and Tate would be buried in the system.

"We don't know what's going to happen." The garlic aroma was soon joined by the tantalizing smell of grilling meat, and Connor glanced over at the church, sending a silent prayer to its patron saints to stop teasing him. "His mother's family signing over custody to us as guardians helps our case, but finding Robinson opens everything up."

"A lot of things would be solved if we could find Robinson," Kane pointed out. "I know a lot of the Narcotics guys would love to get their hands on him. It seems like every place you guys shut down, he finds two more places to cook."

"We had two raids last week, and they thought for sure he would be at one of the spots, but when the team got there, it was cleaner than a confessional." Focusing his attention on his little boy, Connor couldn't help but smile. "I told you Forest signed him up for an art class, right?"

"Only about twenty times," his brother drawled. "How's Picasso doing?"

"Well, we can honestly say that what he lacks in dancing skills, he more than makes up for it with his art." Connor pulled out his phone and began to scroll through his photos. After finding what he was looking for, he leaned over to show Kane. "Tell me that's not a perfect horse. His teacher said he has a really good grasp of musculature and perspective. If he can do this at eight, imagine what he can do when he's an adult."

"If that's what he wants to do," Kane murmured, studying the image.

"Definitely only if that's what he wants to do," Connor replied, sliding back into English. "Did Da tell you Ian quit the force?"

Kane scrubbed a hand over his thick black hair, then nodded. "Last night. I'm not sure what to do. I texted him and told him I support whatever he wants, no matter what that is, but he hasn't replied yet. It's not like we all go out into life to wear a star. He's not the first one to decide being a cop isn't for him."

"No, but think about the other two." Another burst of laughter from the lawn, and this time Kane grew a smile as well. "Quinn and Braeden are both very strong-willed. Even if it is hard to see it sometimes, those two know what they want and to chase after it. Ian's never been like that. He postures and fronts to hide his insecurities. We've seen that before. Sometimes I think he does things because it's what he thinks is expected of him."

"You've got a bit of that going yourself, you know," Kane interjected. "You had a life plan laid down in your head when you were twelve, Con. You know I love Da with all of my soul and heart, but you wanted to grow up to be his mirror. Wife. Bunch of snot nosed kids who looked like you. Maybe a couple of cats. In a lot of ways, you became your own man when you hooked up with Forest."

"I did. At least give me some credit for going SWAT instead of the detective route. I mean, I had to leave something for you." Connor chuckled, remembering how Forest turned his life upside down and how he had to reach inside of himself to find his own way. "As for our baby brother, I sent Ian a text too, but maybe he thinks we are going to try to talk him out of it. It's harder with the youngers, especially Ian and Ryan. I'm not going to say I understand everything he's thinking, but maybe at least I can understand how he feels a little bit. I just don't want him to get lost."

Kane slapped Connor on the shoulder. "Agreed. Maybe we should get together and take him—"

The blast of a backfire thundered through the park as an old Chevy C10 accelerated up the hill leading away from the church. Another press of gas brought another volley, the rapid small booms crackling loudly. The truck jerked once then twice, firing off again before it gained back enough momentum to pick up speed. The driver came to a rolling pause at the stop sign, then hurried through the intersection, pushing the truck hard to make the green light a few yards away. A roll of sharp retorts hammered out of the truck's exhaust system, then quieted down once it went through the second intersection and headed up the hill.

Connor watched the truck fight the hill. "We could be assholes and call that in, but his valves are—"

The hit came hard and fast. Connor took the brunt of Tate's weight to his ribs and chest, the boy's clenched hand smacking Con across the jaw. Tate's slender arms wrapped around Connor's neck, but his legs were uncoordinated and flailing, striking Connor's thighs and shins. The boy's body shook such fierce tremors Connor could barely get his arms around Tate. Pulling his son into his lap, he held on tightly, looking up over the boy's head to make eye contact with Forest, who stood on the lawn a few feet away with a shocked expression on his face and gripping the battered Frisbee in his hands.

"You're okay, *a mhac*. We're all okay." Connor rocked the boy, shifting Tate's weight around until he was cradled in Connor's arms. Dude was on his feet, his pink tongue licking Tate's ankle, but it didn't appear as if the boy even noticed. "What's wrong? What happened?"

Forest crouched next to Connor and placed his hand on Tate's back. "We're right here. Everyone's fine. *You're* fine."

"Probably was the truck." Miki snapped his fingers at Dude, a silent order to leave Tate alone. The dog huffed but stopped his licking. "Scared the fuck out of me for a second. Thought somebody was shooting off a gun."

Tate's hysterical gasps finally broke into sobbing, a few sniffles followed by a smear of wetness on Connor's neck where the boy had his face buried. Tate leaned into the rocking, following the motion with a sway of his shoulders. Forest's eyes glittered with tears; then he rested his forehead on Tate's back, nesting the boy between them.

"Is that what you thought it was? Did you think somebody was shooting a gun?" Connor gently prodded and was rewarded by a short burst of nods, but Tate remained tucked up against him. "You've got to talk to me, kiddo. I can't help you unless I know what you're scared of."

"I thought someone was shooting at us and I got scared," Tate stammered between sobs. His voice was muffled, but his tense body and violent tremors spoke more than his words. "So I found you."

"How's our boy doing?" Connor asked as Forest padded into their bedroom. "Did he go back to sleep?"

Their evening had gone well, or so Forest thought, but at some point in the rainy sullen hours of the morning, something dark cracked open in Tate's mind and released the nightmares corralled there. Whatever sunlight they brought home with them from the park slithered away once sleep took hold of Tate, and when his terrified cries rang through the house, Forest stumbled out of the bed first, telling Connor to keep the blankets warm.

"He did. I got him some cold water to drink, and we talked about how much fun he had today." Forest eased himself onto the bed, working around Connor's sprawled form. "This would be a lot easier if you weren't a hill giant."

The man was huge, taking up a lot of the mattress even when sitting up against the headboard. Trying to find enough clear space to lie down was a problem until Connor looped an arm around Forest's waist and pulled him down on top of his legs. Spreading his knees apart, Connor got Forest settled against him.

"You fit fine right there." Kissing Forest's forehead, he murmured, "But did he go back to sleep?"

"A little bit after he asked if he could have a sleepover. Not with any of the kids he knows," Forest grumbled, adjusting himself so he was sideways against Connor's chest and able to look up into his husband's face. "He wants a sleepover with Dude. He's got about ten thousand friends from school, but he wants his uncles' dog to spend the night."

"You know, we can always get him—"

"Nope. Stop." Forest put his index finger over Connor's lips. "Don't say that. Not now. Not *yet*."

Since the moment Connor rescued Tate, their once steady lives began to churn and rock beneath them, a caustic fluid bubbling with hazards and stiffened in places from age. There were patches of familiar solid ground beneath their feet, but the uncertainty of their future made it impossible to promise their broken-souled son anything permanent.

Connor's throat rumbled with a low growl, and his broad hands gripped Forest's hips, maneuvering him up until the drummer was sitting on Connor's thighs. Flailing at the sudden rearrangement of his body, Forest grabbed at the headboard to give himself some support, sliding his knees to opposite sides of Connor's legs, then resting his ass on his husband's knees.

"I won't say it, but it's something to think about once everything gets signed off and he feels safe." The blue of Connor's eyes was nearly lost in the milky shadows cast by a sconce on the wall. The light played with his features, casting them a golden-tinted cragginess and caressing Connor's strong nose and mouth. His fingers weren't still, exploring the soft skin beneath Forest's T-shirt. Bending his head down, Connor sniffed at Forest's neck, then murmured, "This is nice right now. It's been a long time since we've sat in the quiet together."

Forest laughed and rested his forehead briefly against Connor's. "When was the last time you remember things being quiet? I love the boy, but he is a bit of anxious chaos."

"Reminds me a little bit of you."

"I am the least chaotic person you know," he refuted. "I'll give you the anxious. But just a little bit."

Connor canted his head and remained silent for a good ten seconds, his attention elsewhere. Just when Forest was about to ask if he was okay, Connor's gaze returned to Forest's face. "How sure are you that Tate's asleep?"

Forest straightened up, resting his weight on his husband's legs. "Very sure. He went to the bathroom. Brushed his teeth again. Then started yawning in the middle of him telling me about throwing the baseball with you like I wasn't there to cheer him on or anything."

"He gets excited," Connor replied. "Second question, how closed is that door? All the way closed or cracked a little bit open so we can hear the kid again if we need to?"

Forest knew where Connor was leading the conversation, the not-so-subtle hint of his long fingers easing past the drawstring of Forest's cotton shorts giving him a clue about what Connor was thinking. The scrape of Connor's fingernails along the top of his buttocks' crease let loose a wave of shivers up Forest's spine and down the back of his legs.

"It is very closed." His brain glitched, and for the life of him, Forest couldn't remember a damned thing except it'd been too long since Connor touched him. "Maybe. Probably. Want me to go check?"

Connor craned his neck slightly, peering around Forest. "Looks closed to me. I think we can risk it."

Forest let out a soft scolding *tsk*. "Or I could get off you and go check."

"But I already have you where I need you," Connor growled, the Irish in his words thickening with a husky purr. "Why would I want you to leave?"

Forest ran his hands over Connor's torso, the short soft hair on his husband's chest tickling his palms as he stroked at the curves and planes of muscle beneath Connor's warm skin. Every pass of Connor's fingers along Forest's back and waist flexed his sculpted arms, his biceps going taut when he stretched slightly to caress the curve of Forest's ass. Con's nipples were hard points before Forest circled the left one with his index finger, turning the stroke into a hard flick of his nail then smiling wickedly at the hiss he'd drawn out of his husband's lush mouth.

The thin cotton of Forest's sleep shorts did nothing to mask Connor's thickening cock, its growing length caught between their bodies and the friction of their movements. His own shaft responded, aching slightly when his shorts constricted its swell. Moving forward to ease the fabric loose only made things worse as it dragged the rough inner seam against the velvety sensitive skin of his head.

Connor's mouth captured Forest's in a hard kiss, heating the air between them and leaving Forest panting when they broke apart. A twist of Connor's hips drove Forest down into the mattress, his husband's weight shifting over him as Con stretched for the nightstand. The scent of his cop's skin was too tempting, the mingle of soap and everything else drawing a searing heat up into Forest's belly. Lifting his chin, he pushed slightly against Connor's chest to sink his teeth into the spray of light scars on Con's shoulder, a memento of a time when his brother Kane rescued a hawk.

"Stop distracting me," Connor hissed. "There, got it."

They spent the next few seconds trying to untangle themselves from the clothes twisted around their limbs. What was comfortable and forgiving to sleep in became a cotton prison when trying to work limbs and hard cocks free of stretched fabric. Something tore, but Forest didn't know whose clothing became a victim of their need to have the other's naked body against them. A long, shuddering breath later, nothing mattered anymore but the touch of Connor's oil-slickened finger lightly pressing into him, especially when Forest experienced the simmering burn of his body parting to let Connor in.

"Not going to last long." Forest hated saying it, but he'd never been closer to the truth or edged to the point of release. "Fuck. I'm going to lose it, Con."

It *had* been too long since they'd found any time to be with each other. He didn't realize how much he needed to feel Connor exploring him, delving into him. Clutching at his husband's shoulders, he brought his knees up, wanting more than just a taste of Connor inside of him.

"Just hold on, *a ghra*." Molten desire rolled Connor's voice as he whispered into Forest's parted mouth. "I need to make this good for you."

Connor left him empty, drawing away, but a moment later—a breath filled with the enrapturing scent of Connor's skin being coated with fragrant lube—Forest felt his husband's slick hand under his thigh, lifting it up to rest on Connor's hip. He shifted down, moving his calf up and tilting his hips to meet the head of Connor's shaft looking for a place to seat itself. There was a brief starburst of welcome pain, then the familiar tug of Connor's hand wrapped through Forest's hair, twisting the long strands around his knuckles to tilt Forest's head back into the pillows. Connor's sharp teeth found the soft skin of Forest's neck, and then lightning erupted through Forest's body as Connor pushed himself in.

"Scared to move," Connor grunted against Forest's throat. "The inside of you is like seeing heaven. I can only stand so much, then—"

"Less poetry," he grumbled back, squeezing down around Connor's length. "More fucking."

Connor's chuckle was deep and throaty, a sensual sound that reverberated through Forest's body to wrap around his balls. "*Mar is mian leat, mo aghra.*"

The stretch Connor gave him hadn't been enough, but the catch of Connor's cock against his sensitive skin drove Forest insane. Connor moved his hand from Forest's thigh to the small of his back, leveraging him up a few inches and tilting his hips up enough to change the angle of Forest's core. Thrusting deeper, Connor struck every titillating nerve nestled inside of Forest. He could feel the hard grip Connor had on his back, the press of Con's palm digging into the rise of Forest's asscheek with every downward plunge.

Forest could only hold on. His fingers ached with the effort to remain latched on to Connor's moving shoulders. It was a fierce ride, a reckless steeplechase toward a moment they both knew lay ahead of them but not where they would find it. A thin sheen of sweat coated their stomachs, the slap of wet skin echoing once—maybe twice—then Connor yanked Forest closer, sliding his forearm under Forest to bring them together.

Caught between their undulating bodies, Forest's cock throbbed with the continuous rub. He lost his breath, unable to keep up with Connor's demanding rhythm amid the sparks firing through him. Their moves became frantic, then fell back into a beat Forest could follow, but his skin was already on too tight.

When Connor bent his head down, filling Forest's mouth with hot Irish and a needy tongue, Forest came apart.

If the gush of heat against their bellies as Forest's cock spent his release wasn't enough, then the twisting spasms of his ass clenching down on Connor's shaft should have told the Irish cop he'd brought Forest over the edge. Stiffening in Connor's arms, Forest rode the crashing white shocks filling him, lifting and falling with each wave.

"*A ghra*, I've got you," Connor murmured, cradling Forest as his body reached its zenith. His panting breath shortened into harsh puffs of air, and he buried his face into the crook of Forest's neck, spilling more Irish endearments or curses into the sweat-dampened skin he found there.

A single final thrust pushed Connor's girth into Forest's shaking body, stretching him fully apart and leaving no room for the hot spill of Connor's climax.

Tremors gripped both of their bodies as Connor gently rocked them down out of the heart-shattering rhythm they'd reached. Forest's legs begged to be stretched out, his thighs burning from the strength of Connor's pounding exertions, but he was reluctant to let his husband pull away.

"There is probably going to be a mess when we get off this bed," Forest rumbled, but he wrapped his arms around Connor's neck, prolonging their sticky togetherness.

"What's left of my pants are underneath you, so it won't be too bad." Connor dug his thumbs into the twitching muscles along Forest's thighs, easing some of the spasms. "Shower or baby wipes?"

"Shower. I think I need a lot of hot water and maybe a little bit of soap." Resting his head back against the pillows, Forest gazed up into his husband's warm blue eyes. "And since it seems like the house is still peaceful and quiet—and we probably won't have to change the sheets—if you're really lucky, I might drop that bar of soap."

CHAPTER
TWELVE

"HOW THE hell do we make this much laundry?" Standing in the middle of the living room, Connor took in the piles of clean clothes covering most of the three long sofas set up in a U around a coffee table with a sadistic craving for snagging toes. "He's just a little boy. How does this all happen?"

He was talking to no one, but venting about the overwhelming herculean task of folding everything Forest brought out of the laundry room somehow made him feel better. When he and Kane turned nine and eight, their mother proclaimed at the dinner table that their dirty clothes were now their responsibility. He'd grumbled at the unfairness of that, especially since he was fairly certain none of his other classmates were burdened with that particular chore, and when he voiced that opinion out loud while scooping mashed potatoes onto his plate, he then earned the elite privilege of having to wash Quinn's laundry as well.

Connor knew he wasn't the smartest Morgan at that table, but he knew he was the one who always was quick to learn a life lesson or two. Speaking out against the unfairness of chores was a stupid mistake, but his frustration was more about the seemingly impossible task of working a washer and dryer while somehow figuring out the magical separation ritual his mother performed on every bit of laundry.

Brigid walked them through the procedure and oversaw them for a few weeks before cutting their leashes. Thankfully, Kane pitched in with Quinn's laundry, because the third Morgan child couldn't stand for anything to be worn twice, whereas he and Kane quickly discovered if a shirt didn't smell bad, it could sit on the back of a chair to be worn again.

Now faced with an almost familiar mountain of boy's clothes to tackle, Connor realized his mother passing on the task of their laundry wasn't just so they could learn independence. Counting off his fingers and figuring out the time spans, he reckoned Brigid had the twins and Braeden to clean up after, as well as herself and Donal.

"I get it now, Mum," he murmured at the ceiling, casting an exasperated, unheard thanks to his mother, a few miles away. "I would have just said fuck it and dressed all of us in black to be done with it."

"It kind of worries me when I come into a room and you're talking to Brigid like she's here," Forest remarked, looking around the living room as if expecting to see Con's diminutive mother lurking in some shadowy corner. "I got Tate's sheets in the dryer and most of the towels in the wash. And to show you how much I love you, I'll even help fold."

"Your generosity knows no bounds," he grumbled back. Forest lifted an eyebrow at him but said nothing as he cleared a space to sit down. With the coffee table cleaned off to hold completed stacks of laundry, Connor sat on the couch across of Forest then grabbed an empty laundry basket to put aside for rolled socks and underwear. "And I know I can't lay any blame on the kid. We *are* doing a lot more outside now that he's living with us."

"Sports, I get. You guys all grew up beating the hell out of each other with balls and bats, so I guess I expected the grass stains and road rash." Forest held up a ratty large boy's T-shirt with what was once a silkscreened fish leaping out of the water on it. "But I wasn't ready for all of you guys to come home with fish guts smeared into your clothes."

Not a lot of the graphic remained intact, but there was enough left to see its original owner got it near Lough Leane many years ago, and in its lifetime, it probably had been worn by more than a few Morgan children. Connor stretched over and grabbed the shirt, plucking it from Forest's grasp. He'd been twelve when Granddad Finnegan took them into a bait shack at Lakes of Killarney, then tossed the rust-colored shirt into the pile of food and drinks he'd gathered up for another day of their weeklong fishing trip. It was the first time Connor was allowed to join the Finnegan men on their yearly trek to the lakes, and he'd pulled a monster salmon the day before, overshadowing everyone else's catch. His granddad wasn't much of a talker—not like his daughter, Brigid— but the shirt had been a trophy of sorts, along with the long brag he told the shopkeeper and a few other fishermen standing near the counter.

The shirt was a piece of sentiment Connor held on to, and at times even loaned out to his siblings, but it always remained in his possession.

Until a few days ago when he pulled it out of the bottom of his dresser drawer and gave it to Tate to wear after telling him the story about how he'd gotten it and what the shirt meant to him.

"Are you going to put that back in the dresser until the next time you guys go fishing?" Forest tackled another nest of socks, separating them out into pairs. "Make sure I got all of the fish smell out of it if you do, because that entire duffel bag was rank."

Connor sniffed the shirt, smelling only fabric softener and soap. Folding it carefully, he said, "No. It's Tate's now. I'll put it in his laundry basket to put away with the rest of his stuff."

As stupid as it sounded, sitting in the living room and sorting clothes was a happiness Connor realized he needed. The house was as quiet as an old Victorian could be, the brisk wind outside testing the strength of the mature trees around the property. Despite the bluster, the skies were crystal blue and without a hint of a threatening cloud anywhere to be seen. They'd woken up with the chickens to get their son off to school, and after a leisurely breakfast, they both agreed tackling a few household chores together to be a good use of Connor's day off.

His belly still full from breakfast, Connor was beginning to get other ideas. Glancing at the clock on the wall, he asked, "What time does Tate's school end today?"

"Three." The level of suspicion in Forest's expression was uncalled for, and Connor almost said something about it, but then Forest asked, "Why?"

"Well, the boy's not here and…." Connor leaned across the coffee table until his lips were almost on Forest's mouth. Surprisingly, Forest didn't pull away, especially considering that his expression deepened into skepticism. "I was thinking we could take a couple of hours and you know…."

Connor knew he would never get tired of the taste of Forest in his mouth. As he pushed in for a kiss, Connor teased Forest's lips open with his tongue, licking and nibbling until Forest responded. Resting his right knee on the table, Connor let it take his weight and slid one of his hands beneath the thick silken fall of Forest's long hair. Deepening their kiss, Connor explored his husband's mouth in a slow, leisurely caress, then captured Forest's moan when Connor rasped his thumb down Forest's throat.

Pulling back just enough to give Forest some air, he dropped his voice to a low rumble. "So what do you think? Feel like taking a nap?"

People often looked at Forest's lanky form and oversized T-shirts and probably thought he was no match for Connor's toned muscular form. What they didn't take into account was the countless hours of precise drumming and the core strength Forest developed over years of playing. The punch he gave Connor's left shoulder stung with every minute Forest spent banging at those skins.

Drawing back, Connor rubbed at his smarting spot and grinned. "What did you think I was talking about?"

Forest bared his teeth back in an exaggerated snarl. "Finish folding the clothes, and then I am going to dig up the filthiest jobs that need to be done around here and put you to work."

"I can think of a lot of filthy things to do to you, love," he growled back. "For instance—"

A hard knock on their front door broke the mood. The rapid tapping was closely followed by a press against the doorbell, the house's refurbished chimes harmonizing its quick medley to announce visitors. The frown on Forest's face and his glance toward the front door was enough to tell Connor his husband wasn't expecting anyone, and since it was his day off, most of his family would treat the morning hours as sacred as a faerie circle they stumbled upon while roaming through the woods.

"If those aren't Girl Scout cookies, I'll send them on their way," Connor promised, tapping his finger on the tip of Forest's nose. "Keep track of where we were. I'll come right back to it."

The doorbell sang again before Connor got to the foyer. Peering through the peephole, he was surprised to find an officious woman in an ill-fitting pink floral suit with two uniformed police officers bookending her as she stood on the porch. A flood of possibilities of why they were there rapid-fired through his mind, but none of the scenarios he imagined didn't have a phone call attached to them.

Forest came up behind him. "Who is it?"

"I don't know, but she's got a couple of cops with her." Connor unlocked the door, then turned the knob. "Let's see what they want."

The woman's pinched face looked familiar, but Connor couldn't place her. A slight grunt from Forest said he did. She crept her thin lips into a smile, ratcheting up the corners in measured mechanical increments until a bit of her teeth were showing. Behind her, the cops were seasoned with at least ten years on the job under their belt. They shifted uncomfortably in their polished black shoes, regretful expressions on both of their faces.

"Can we come in to talk to you, Lieutenant Morgan? And your husband too." She nodded her head at Forest, where he was pressed up against Connor's right arm. "This is about Tate Robinson. I don't think you and I have met, but I'm Stephanie Young, one of the caseworkers assigned to Tate's case."

"Come in. We were just doing laundry," Connor replied. Forest broke away toward the living room, scrambling to clear the couches of unfolded clothes by dumping the sorted piles into any empty basket he could find. "Can I get you some coffee or tea? Water?"

"No, thank you. We will try to be as quick as possible and get out of your way." Stepping up into the house, Young teetered on her high heels for a brief moment then straightened up quickly, clenching the red accordion file she brought with her tightly against her body.

The cops' nameplates were Baker and Hernandez, obviously partners who'd spent a lot of time together, judging by the symbiotic body language they had coming through the door. Neither one of them was fresh out of the academy, but Hernandez looked to be Baker's junior by a few years, judging by the heavy dash of salt threaded through Baker's thick brown hair. Hernandez acknowledged Connor with a quick respectful nod, but Baker lingered for a brief second.

"I'm sorry about this, Lieutenant," the man muttered under his breath. "Neither one of us wants to do this, but CPS is pulling the strings."

Despite the cleared-off couches, no one was sitting. Instead, Forest sat on the arm of the couch closest to the front door while Young squared off in a spot across the coffee table. Hernandez stood quietly near the arch between the foyer and the living room, looking as if he would rather have a root canal then be standing behind the tightly wound caseworker. Connor followed Baker in, slightly surprised to receive another one of Young's clockwork-movement smiles. With her light brown hair scraped back from her thin face into a severe bun at the back of her skull and her insincere but practiced expressions, she resembled a jewelry box ballerina freed from her lacquered prison but still missing the spring that held her there.

Standing next to Forest, Connor placed his hand on the back of the couch, leaning into his husband. "How can we help you?"

"I'm here to inform you that, as of half an hour ago, Child Protective Services resumed custody of the minor, Tate Robinson. The officers were brought as a precaution—"

"You took him?" Through their touch, Connor felt Forest's heart, pounding in panic, stutter. "Con...."

The drummer was nearly halfway out of his seat before Connor could lay a hand on his shoulder to keep him still. Baker and Hernandez had already closed the distance between them and the caseworker before Forest's words left his mouth.

"It's okay," Connor reassured the cops, holding up a hand to keep them back. "*A ghra*, let her finish and find out what's going on first."

He was trying to maintain his composure, but it was hard with the hot raging emotions cutting through his soul and heart. Connor's mind was lit up with anger, and his thoughts grew dark and violent. Cutting, harsh words floated over his tongue, pushing to get out, but the tiny kernel of rational brain he had left cautioned him against ripping into the caseworker.

She'd taken his son—their son—and throttling the woman carrying that message wasn't going to do them any good. Forest's panic rushed over them, a tsunami of fury and loss, but he couldn't afford to let himself get swept up by it. Con needed to stay strong for both of them, at least long enough to hear Young out so he could begin to fix things and bring Tate home.

No matter what had happened—or how it happened—Tate was going to come home.

"Sir...." Hernandez frowned slightly, keeping his voice to a low calm. "Mr. Ackerman, we're just here to make sure everything stays safe and nothing escalates to endanger anyone. So please, help us all out, okay?"

Rationally, Connor knew exactly why the cops were there. It was a volatile situation, one he'd walked into himself more than a few times, and too often, a few hot words set off a powder keg of violence. He'd picked through the pieces of too many domestic disturbances gone wrong and covered his SFPD badge with a strip of black tape to mourn a fallen officer. Baker and Hernandez knew what they were walking into—a SWAT lieutenant with a variety of heavy-duty weapons in the house. They were gambling that Connor would keep a cool head or, better yet, followed protocol and locked up his guns and ammo.

Baker shot him a look of extreme relief when Connor pressed Forest back down again, but neither cop took a step back.

"If they took him from school, he doesn't have anything." Forest's eyes were wild with dread. "How could you just take him? Stice promised that would never happen."

"She did," Connor replied, but he kept his gaze on Young. "And she sure as hell wouldn't go and do this without telling us first."

He'd trusted Stice. They all did. Everyone in the family had jumped through every flaming hoop CPS put up in front of them. Connor knew there was always a chance they would lose Tate to the system, but the possibility of it lessened with each day he spent with them. Or at least that's what they'd been told.

Swallowing the bile rising up his throat, Connor stroked Forest with his thumb, anchoring himself as best he could by touching the man he loved.

After exhaling a deep breath, Forest spoke, his tone high with raw anger. "I don't understand why you guys removed him. It doesn't make any fucking sense. He's doing well here. He's been with us for months. He's finally beginning to feel safe. Like he has a home. Why is she doing this to him? To us?"

"What do we have to do to change her mind?" Connor interjected, flattening his words as much as he could to not agitate Young. The woman had tensed up, an animated cardboard sentinel devoid of empathy and compassion, as she tore their family apart. "If she ordered this, she can rescind this."

"Deputy Director Stice can't counteract a judge's order." Young opened the folder she'd been holding, rifling through its contents before drawing out a thick packet held together with a black binder clip. "As I was trying to say, the department removed him at the school site without notification because there was concern that you and your husband are flight risks."

"Bullshit," Forest snapped back. "And why would we take him now after we done everything by the book? *Your* book."

"Lieutenant Morgan is a dual citizen of the United States and the Republic of Ireland, I believe," the caseworker pointed out. "You, Mr. Ackerman, belong to a musician group with access to a private jet, and you have enough financial influence to travel at a moment's notice.

"Those were all factors in the judge's decision. Tate's case came up on the Family Court docket, and the presiding judge wants him to be independently evaluated over the next few weeks." She set the packet of papers down on the coffee table, sliding a corner under a small stack of T-shirts Forest left behind. "Normally the child would remain with the family, but there are extenuating circumstances, such as whether or not the father listed on his birth certificate retains any right to the minor and whether or not it would be in the child's best interest to place him with a family outside of his ethnicity. All of those factors, including the flight risk, necessitated a removal from the custody home and a placement with a foster family until a ruling can be made regarding his status."

Forest's hand reached up to grab at Connor's, his fingers scrambling to find purchase. Clasping their hands together, Connor asked, "Are we going to be allowed to see him during this? We've made plans with him to do things with our family—his family—and... I'm sorry, but this isn't right."

"You just yanked him away from everything he has here. He feels safe here, and you are just taking that away from him." Forest's agitation drove him to his feet despite Connor's hand holding his. The cops exchanged glances, heavy with anticipation, so Connor tugged Forest back. Turning slightly, Forest snapped, "How the fuck are you okay with this? They took our kid!"

The despair in Forest's voice broke Connor, and he pulled his husband close, wrapping his arms around Forest. It was a fight of wills, but a moment later, Forest surrendered and relaxed into Connor's embrace, the tears glittering in his hurt brown eyes dampening Connor's shirt.

"I'm not okay with this, babe," Connor whispered into Forest's hair. "But we need to know what's going on so we can fight this. Because as soon as we get this woman out of our house, you and I are going to get Tate back. Even if I have to burn the world down to do it."

CHAPTER THIRTEEN

THE UPSTAIRS bedroom at the back of the house still smelled faintly of little boy. The walls were plastered with art and posters, including a very familiar and particularly treasured one of Forest and his band lounging against a graffiti dragon painted on the wall in Chinatown. Everything was put away, toys and belongings stashed into nooks and crannies, and the computer with its drawing software squatted in standby mode beneath Tate's empty desk.

The staccato taps and bites of conversation rose up from downstairs, climbing toward the fragile silence Forest immersed himself in. His home had become a war room of legal arguments and injunctions, his world suddenly filled with tangled red tape and people in expensive suits.

He should be grateful. Within minutes of the door closing behind the caseworker who'd ripped their lives apart, a few phone calls rallied everyone they knew to a strange battlefield. Overwhelmed, Forest didn't know where they would even begin to fight, but strangely enough, Damien stepped in and took charge. If ever there was a question of Crossroads Gin being his family—his own band of brothers—it was answered when the group's leader reached out to their manager, Edie, and fired up a legal department Forest wasn't even aware existed.

"Trust me, honey," Edie's raspy voice echoed over that first video call. "I work in the entertainment industry. My company has an entire legal division dedicated to custody battles. This case is going to be like throwing a single sardine into a pit of ravenous gators. I hope that judge has a lot of clean underwear because he is going to be going through them really quickly."

And oddly enough, Damien again chimed in, suggesting Edie go in with a velvet glove over any iron fist she brought down. It was enlightening to see Damie filling out a role he had for the band, but Forest had never seen him in action. There was a steeliness to his posture when he leaned forward to Edie, laying out a course of action to bring Tate home but also keeping everyone aware of the Morgans' law enforcement positions. They couldn't afford to make any enemies in the judicial system, Damien cautioned. The lawyers would have to step delicately around egos so as not to endanger any future interactions Connor or any of the others might have within the court system. This wasn't the time or place for a scorched-earth offensive, he warned. Bringing Tate home quickly was their objective, but if possible, they needed to stave off a nuclear apocalypse unless absolutely necessary.

It'd been an icy splash of cold water across Forest's nerves, and now a week into the fight, he fully understood what Damien meant. There were lines being drawn across hot sands he didn't know existed, and every hour seemed to bring a different complication or more paperwork until he was drowning in a sea of confusion. Even now, with three of what seemed like the most expensively dressed people he'd ever seen sitting downstairs in his living room drinking soda and hammering out agreements with everybody even remotely connected to the case, Forest felt like he was a piece of driftwood caught in a frantic whirlpool he couldn't escape.

A knock on the room's doorframe broke Forest out of his fugue. Looking up, he was gifted with one of Brigid's warm smiles. At some point in the last hour or so, she'd shed her heels and now walked barefoot through the Victorian, a curvaceous pixie with a riot of flame-red hair bobbing through a sea of tall men. She kept her large brood in line with a sharp tongue and a generous heart, extending her maternal embrace to include her sons' husbands and lovers.

And Forest thanked any God in existence that she counted him as one of her favorites.

"Can I come in, *a thaisce*?" The Irish lilt on her words was a bit rougher than Donal's, flavored with a hint of wild salty seas and busy ports than her husband's softer country tones. While they both still carried a deep love for their homeland, Brigid was more than likely to fall into Gaelic compared to the Irish cop she'd followed to America. "Or do you want to be alone?"

"No, come in," he replied, shifting down on the bed to give her more room to sit. "It was just getting too loud downstairs. So I came up here to... *not* think."

Her toenails were painted a glittery bright blue, an odd choice considering her fingernails were clean of polish. He must've looked perplexed because Brigid glanced down at her feet and laughed before sitting down. Stretching out her legs, she wiggled her toes.

"I always make a mess of my feet when I do my toenails, and I swear if anyone even looks at them, I'm so ticklish I start laughing, so no pedicures for me," she murmured as if sharing a deep dark secret. "And then I married someone who is very meticulous, and it's something Donal does for me while we hide away from the world and share a spot of whiskey."

"I never knew that," he confessed, his imagination straining to conjure up an image of Connor's heavily muscled father crouching over his tiny wife's foot to paint her delicate toes. "Does he like doing that?"

"He does." She nodded and tucked her feet underneath her rather than let them dangle over the edge of the bed. "Just like I love to sit on the bathroom counter and shave his face. There were—and still are— times when we hardly ever saw each other, so we would take whatever minutes we had with each other and just do small little things like painting toenails or maybe a quick dance in the kitchen."

"I wish...." Exhaustion stole away Forest's thoughts, and he stumbled over his own tongue. "I don't know what I'm saying anymore. I feel like the last couple of days I've just been talking to... I didn't realize how hard and cold silence could be. And I feel so fucking stupid for saying it, but even when he was at school, it was like a part of him was still here filling out the quiet."

"You're not stupid or crazy," Brigid reassured him, rubbing at his thigh. "Children leave a resonance behind in the house, echoes of their dreams and arguments. It makes sense that you would miss that. You are a musician, an artist of sounds. Of course you are going to miss his noise."

Surrounded by Tate's belongings, Forest's skin crawled with an unsettling dread. Resting his elbows on his thighs, he clasped his hands together, anything to stop his fingers from shaking. "The caseworker... I'm so fucking angry, Birdie. She wouldn't let us even pack clothes for him. I've never wanted to punch somebody so much in my entire life. He's out there with who the fuck knows and probably thinks we just threw him out. We worked so hard to—"

Everything Forest had held in since CPS removed Tate from their home broke through the brittle control he had over his anger and sorrow. The sour reek of his stomach's contents burned the roof of his mouth, and he fought not to soil the rug covering the room's hardwood floor. Choking, he fell into a fit of coughing, his eyes stinging with unshed tears as Brigid pounded at his back.

"Let me get you some water," she entreated. "Just try to breathe deeper. Thank God you spoiled the boy and put a mini fridge in here for drinks."

"He forgets and gets dehydrated," Forest spat out between coughs. "Apparently it makes him cool with his friends."

Brigid returned with a small water bottle chilled to nearly freezing. "So a mini fridge makes him cool but not his SWAT commando and rock star parents?"

"No," Forest croaked, cracking the water bottle open. "All that gets us is the school cranking me up for money and donations while packs of soccer-mom hyenas descend on Connor when he goes to pick up the kids."

The water helped chase the bitterness away from Forest's mouth. He sipped slowly, letting it warm on his tongue before swallowing to keep his stomach from roiling at the cold. The indistinct chatter from downstairs continued to rise and fall, punctuated by an occasional phone ringing, but it was nothing Forest could make out.

"It'll be okay." Brigid settled down on the bed again, facing Forest as she crossed her legs. "I know it's hard right now. But we will get through this."

"I'm just scared he thinks he's been abandoned." Forest shut his eyes briefly, trying to dismiss the gut-wrenching panic he fought every time he thought about CPS taking Tate out of his school. "It's just so out of our control. I don't know what anyone said to him. If he even understands what's really going on. I just wish we could talk to him. Tell him were fighting for him."

He kept coming back to that hopelessness that rose up without even a hint of summoning. Forest lost count of how many nightmares they'd chased away from Tate's sleep and if the terrors returned because he and Connor weren't there to keep them back. There were things the little boy refused to speak about, including his mother and the life they'd led in the filth Robinson mired them in. Still, there were signs Forest recognized from his own experiences, and he hated for Tate to carry those stains on his soul.

"We have to have faith," she consoled, *tsk*ing when Forest flashed her an askance glance. "Don't you be looking at me like that, son. I'm not talking about faith in God or angels. I'm talking about you having a belief that you've done right by the boy and that he has faith in you. He knows the two of you. He looks for you when he has doubts. He runs to you when he's scared. And now that he's been taken by someone and not allowed to speak to you, you have to trust that he knows deep in his heart that you will come for him because he's your child. Believe me, I have a bit of experience with feral children and their broken faith."

"What do you say? From your mouth to God's ears?" Forest chuckled despite the shadows burdening him. "I don't want him to lose hope. Young—the caseworker that came here—said it was going to be three weeks but—they were talking about months downstairs."

"Now you're borrowing trouble," Brigid warned. "The lawyer was talking about worst-case scenario and that they were going to fight to make sure that wasn't the situation. I know it's easy to fall into every dark hole you find, but that's not going to do you or Connor any good."

The downstairs chatter suddenly rose to a cacophony of tangled shouts and hoots. It struck quickly and out of nowhere, and the noise was startling, a thunderstorm captured within the Victorian's too-solemn walls. Before Forest could even catch his breath, heavy footsteps thumped up the stairs, and Connor's broad frame filled the doorway a moment later.

They stared at each other, caught in an amber moment of their lives. It was going to be a memory Forest knew he would carry always. Sometimes a definitive slice of something momentous dug down into the granite and etched out a forever mark into his bones. He drank in everything he saw, from Connor's beautiful face and the easy grace of his long-limbed body poised at the doorway of Tate's room. Worry still tattooed a drawn sparseness to Connor's features, but his expression was lighter, nearly a beatific glow when his mouth quirked into a smile at seeing Forest sitting on the bed.

His husband prowled across the floor, moving quickly in a quiet stalk. The drawn-out look on his face, a shattered restlessness both of them woke up with, was gone, burned away by his bright smile and warm blue eyes. Catching Forest's face in his hands, Connor stole Forest's breath away in a deep kiss, as forceful as the rapid percussive beat his heart kicked up in his chest.

Leaving Forest panting when he pulled back, Connor's grin grew even wider. "They got a judge. In Family Court. She's going to hear our injunction request three days from now. We've got three days to get everything together, but we got in, babe. It's just a first step, but it's a big one."

THE HOUSE was quiet again, but oddly enough, it still seemed to echo with half-remembered conversations and staggered thoughts. Slumped down in the corner of the living room's longest couch, Connor watched with hooded eyes as Forest paced in front of the bay window, his eyes settling on nothing and lost in reflection. The air retained a slight hint of Chinese food, a heavy box of delectable noodles and other dishes from a favorite restaurant on Grant Street courtesy of his brother Braeden. He hadn't been hungry until he bit into the crispy *gau gee* Brigid forced on him; then it became a battle not to shove everything into his mouth. A few sparse leftovers now resided in their fridge, and everything but the paperwork on their dining room table was cleaned up and put away. His head throbbed from lack of sleep and too much stimulus, but Connor felt for the first time since Tate was taken that he could breathe without his ribs digging into his heart.

"Come here," Connor called out to Forest as he slapped the couch cushion. "I need to cuddle my husband."

"Your husband is burping up chow fun. You squeeze too hard and my guts are going to explode out like a sea cucumber's." Grumbling a bit, Forest padded over, then flopped down against Connor, fitting himself into the curve of Con's shoulder and arm. "My ears are ringing. I play in a rock band, and you guys were so loud I think I lost my hearing."

Connor scoffed. "Tonight was nothing. Try growing up with seven brothers and sisters. It's like trying to have a conversation in a wind tunnel."

Forest stared off into nothing again, then tilted his head back to look at Connor. "Your mom must have wanted to kill every single one of you."

"There were some days I would've done it for her," he confessed wryly. "It's not like we were bad kids, but you've got that many hot-tempered Irish spawn confined in a house on a rainy day and you'd be surprised at how quickly murder floats to the top of your to-do list."

It was Forest's turn to laugh. "She's always telling me you guys were angels."

"She must've been drunk, because a lot of what I remember is everyone fighting." He had fun memories of his childhood, including the sometimes-bloody battles he had with his younger siblings. "That is mostly what kids do, especially if there are a lot of them. We fought and threw things and kicked each other. It was easier for me and Kane as we were the oldest, but that also meant if one of the kids screwed up, we were the ones who they came around to fix it so Mum or Da didn't find out. And it wasn't just us eight. Sionn and Rafe were in the middle of it too. Both of them practically lived there. But God help the sorry bastard who even thought about raising a hand to one of us. Sometimes I think we spent so much time fighting with each other because it was practice for the times we would have to throw punches to protect our own."

"A bunch of savages," Forest scolded lightly. "Hey, did you know that your dad paints your mom's toenails?"

"Yep. I think I found out that most men don't do that for their wives when I was thirteen. I was sleeping over at a friend's house, and there was a movie we were watching where a man did that for his girlfriend, and my friend's mom laughed and said no guy ever does that."

"Did you tell her about Donal?"

"Yeah, but I don't think she believed me." Cradling Forest tighter against him, Connor brushed a kiss on the back of Forest's head. "It wasn't like I didn't know people have different childhoods than I did. I mean, Sionn and Rafe were right there. But I guess if I thought about it, my parents showed me what being married was like, so I guess I figured everyone had what they have."

Forest twisted slightly again, glancing up at Connor. "And now?"

Connor teased a smile out of Forest's full mouth with a nibbling kiss at the corner of his lips. "Now I know that everybody makes marriage their own. It's work. And a lot of talking. A little bit of compromise, sometimes. But mostly it's about listening. I have to be better at that for you. Sometimes I hear what you say and I'm hearing it with my ears— *my experience*—and not through your perspective."

"I do the same thing," Forest murmured. "Sometimes I look at what you do and I try to figure out how you got there in your head, but I just can't."

"I don't mind if you ask me what the fuck I'm doing." Snug against Forest's warmth, the twisting pressure of the day was finally leaving Connor's body. "Sometimes it's good to kick me that way. I have a bad habit of doing first then explaining later."

"Most of the time, I just figure you know what you're doing. Sometimes, though, I do ask." His husband snorted. "Like the time you kept buying boxes of salt every time you went to the store. After the fourth one, I figured you were doing some weird science experiment and just forgot to tell me."

"No, that was just me working too many hours." Tilting his head back to rest against the couch, Connor pointed out, "We did use a lot of it to make that salt-crusted miso salmon with Tate. He got a kick out of it. We'll have to do that again when he comes home."

It was as if Connor broke some mystical seal and let loose the Horsemen of the Apocalypse. Forest stiffened into a nearly rigid blank, and the tension between them rose up hard and fast. Hooking his arm down, Connor stroked at Forest's sternum with a gentle brush of his fingers, coaxing his husband to settle down.

"He's going to come home," Forest whispered, nearly frantic with intensity. "I never thought I could miss someone this much. And I feel like I let him down. I failed him when he needed me the most because I couldn't stop them from taking him."

"Me too," Connor whispered gently. "And I know it was out of our control. Maybe that's what pisses us both off the most. It's one thing for us to do everything right and for someone to say we're not good enough, but to take him from us without giving us a chance to tell him we love him is screwed up. We are damn fucking good for that kid, and he's ours. All the good. All the bad."

"I just hope he wants to come home." Sniffing loudly, Forest worked back into the crook of Connor's body. "Because if you and I are pissed, he's probably raging… or hurt."

"Three days, *a ghra*, and then we'll at least have some kind of idea about what we're up against." Connor gave his husband a gentle push to ease him off the couch. "Right now, it's late and we both should go to bed. You have a snowball's chance in hell of me painting your nails because I suck at it, but if you're really good, I could be talked into giving you a foot massage."

Forest gave him a strange look as he straightened up, stretching out his arms in front of him. "I love you—very much—but I'm really beginning to fucking wonder about you and your family's thing about feet."

CHAPTER FOURTEEN

"YOU SURE you want to do this, Lieutenant?" Yamamoto adjusted one of the straps of his raid gear, aligning the seams of his Kelvar vest. "Captain said you could sit this one out, and we don't mind covering."

"If I don't keep busy, I'm going to go crazy," Connor replied, making one last check on his weapons. "Besides, we're going to need every team member going in, what with the DA's office wanting to hit all of these drug labs at the same time today. It makes sense from a tactical standpoint, but it stretches us out pretty thin. Just be careful and don't pull a Conway."

"You fall through one rotted porch three years ago and people still bring it up," Conway muttered from a few feet away, her eyebrows knitted together in a fierce scowl.

"You fell through the porch headfirst," Yamamoto snapped back with a wicked grin. Putting his gloved fist up so she could see it, he flashed the officer a peace sign, then furiously wiggled his fingers. "Your stubby little legs thrashing in the air? That's never not going to be funny."

"Just watch your back there, buddy," she teased. "One good kick when you're on top of the roof and we'll see how your legs look going down."

The snarky banter and rough teasing were a balm on Connor's tight nerves. It felt good to have his tactical gear on, even better to have something to do to keep his mind off the seemingly endless minutes between his family and the judge who would decide his future. His mother thought he was insane, but his father understood Connor's need to do something—anything—to keep his blood moving. Working a raid was familiar, even with the potential for danger riding on the edge of its perimeter. He wasn't blind to the fact that he would rather face a den of armed criminals than go home to an empty house and devastated husband, but Forest agreed Connor should work the job.

Or rather, Forest threatened to take Connor's testicles off with a pair of nail clippers if he didn't get the fuck out of the house and do something besides hover.

Getting shot at seemed like a better alternative than the nail clippers.

The district attorney's office planned for five hits, the locations spaced out through the city, hoping to break apart a drug pipeline that seemed to spring up overnight. Sectioned out among the various teams, each target was the hub for a particular function in the criminals' supply chain. Connor's squad was tagged for a storage facility, an alleged distribution point for portioned-out meth cooked somewhere off-site. Moving the drugs around was a dangerous risk for the group to take, but it was a necessary precaution considering how many people had a hand in creating the supply. Between the enormous amount of drugs floating around the different sites and the intake of money from selling it, the invested parties had to have been running anxious and paranoid. If just one of them decided to become a bottleneck in the system, everything would go to shit and the city would have a war on its hands.

It had been a treacherous balancing act to decide when they could hit their targets. It wasn't enough just to remove the drugs off the street. The DA also had to strike at the distributors and their pipeline. Word came down of a major delivery—one large enough to export half to Los Angeles—and the already nervous cooperative ratcheted up its mistrust, bringing in all the heavy hitters to oversee the load personally.

"I hate hitting warehouses," Yamamoto grumbled, looking over Connor's shoulder as he examined the schematics again. "There's always shit in there that you didn't know about, or someone decides to throw up a couple of walls when you think you're going into an open space."

"Agreed," Connor murmured. Tracing a section of the warehouse's wall with a stylus, Connor circled an odd thinner section near a line of what looked like portioned-off areas for offices. "I wish someone had taken a recon of the alleyway behind that wall. I want to know if this is an opening of some kind."

"City planner said it was the fuse box." His second-in-command leaned closer, peering at the screen. "Is that as zoomed in as it gets?"

"Yeah. Whoever did these plans wasn't very good at it." Connor tapped at different portions of the warehouse's main floor. "I think we should go in with the idea that it's a breach in the wall of some kind. I'd rather be wrong than sorry. Martinez said they've got six heavies in there but at least eight workers. With the amount of junk supposed to be moving in there tonight, you'd think they would pitch those numbers up."

"Six guys with automatic weapons is enough for me, thank you very much." Yamamoto glanced over his shoulder toward the eerily silent squad prepping around them. "They're probably going hard on guns with the transport."

"That's what I'd do," he agreed. "I'm just wondering how they are processing their distribution. The last thing we need is for runners to be showing up to grab product while we're trying to shut the place down. Yeah, I know that we've talked out all of our options, but I would feel better if we had more uniforms closing in on the perimeter after we go in. If there are runners who break, I'd want them to get caught up in a net outside."

"We just have to depend upon our brothers—and sisters—in blue." Yamamoto slapped at his SWAT insignia emblazoned over his chest. "Me? I like the black. It's slimming."

Coordinating multiple citywide operations was sometimes a tactical nightmare, but Connor knew he could only focus on his own squad, running the raid as tightly to schedule as possible. A grouping of heavy-branched trees in a darkened park kept the SWAT transport vehicles in deep shadows, but with every second that passed, the risk of somebody outside spotting them then alerting anyone in the warehouse grew exponentially. His team was itching to go in, probably running over scenarios in their heads as a way to keep mentally alert. There wasn't a start time. The team wasn't even sure they would be going in. Everything was dependent upon a small group of people in a conference room or stake-out van arguing over whether or not it was an optimal time to do their hits.

As much as his father, Donal, spoke about the chief's efforts to cut back on department bureaucracy, waiting for a raid call to drop was one of those times when Connor was very aware of how political the upper echelon was. For some, it was all about how big of a fish they could catch in their net. It made sense on a lot of levels. Snag the planners, the leaders, and break the system down from the top, but there always seemed to be somebody else ready to step into their place, and in the meantime, the streets were getting dirtier with people's ruined lives.

"You know what my uncle told me the other day?" Yamamoto leaned against the transport's door, hooking his thumbs into the armholes of his vest. "He said it's easier for us to be cops than it was when he was wearing the star. Back then—and he really said that—he hated busting people for pot because it's about the same as alcohol. He thinks we should be happy that the drug busts we're doing are clear and solid. No question about whether we're screwing up some college kid's life because we caught him with a roach clip and a couple of leaves."

"I can understand his point. I just sometimes think we're moving on some targets that could have been handled differently or we're holding on targets that—if we took them down—would do a neighborhood a lot of good. I want to see that change. But I don't think it's going to happen unless...." Connor nodded, catching himself doing an automatic head count of his team. "I'm going to age out of this unit in a few years—"

"Fuck you, Morgan," his friend spat. "I've been in the gym with your father. Shit, I've been there when Kane and the twins were there. You're still going to be fucking running the squad while I float my false teeth in a glass of cleansing bubbly water."

"Morgan, do you copy?" Connor's communication relay crackled. Giving a quick acknowledgment, he waited for the strike team coordinator to respond, tilting his head toward the audio device attached to a shoulder strap on his vest. "Entry is a go. Move your team in at your discretion within the next three. Contact if you need to abort."

"Copy that," he replied, then thumbed the device off. "Okay, Yamamoto, you heard the man. Let's go knocking on some doors."

"Got it, Lieutenant." The officer shot Connor a snappy salute that bordered on sarcastic. "I'll go start the engines."

Connor took a few seconds to touch base with the tactical tech overseeing their coordination. As their newest addition to the team, Chang would have to carry them through every bit of communication, giving them a heads-up of everyone's position as well as any incoming threats. She listened intently to Connor's last-minute instructions, including his caution about the possible door near the offices. Signing off on her readiness, he snagged his helmet from a seat, then settled it over his head, adjusting the comm links.

Three low-pitched beeps verified he was live on their channel; then Connor stepped toward the field.

"Go in low," he said over the team's link. "Get into place, and once I hear everyone's sound-off, I'll give the go. Watch your sixes."

Their target was a throwback from when cheap goods were rubber-stamped through customs but needed a storage facility before they could be trucked out of the city. Most of the industrial area was filled with buildings constructed out of quick slabs, concrete poured sheaths set into place around a central parking lot. The majority of the buildings' entrances were bay doors set into the long sides of a building with a reversed incline ramp for a truck to back its trailer down, bringing its loading space at level with the warehouse floor. However, every single one of them boasted a regular entrance, usually at the far corner of the building, away from the docking area.

The warehouse had a few grimy windows set up high on the front of the building, and according to the plans, a mirror reflection of the same on the backside overlooking a narrow alley. With a quarter of the team set to cover the main doors in case the warehouse's workers decided to run out that way, Connor and the rest of his team focused on a broad metal door. Someone with challenged spelling skills and an unsteady hand had painted the word *Offise* across its slightly battered surface.

Connor made a sweep of the area, making sure the coast was clear. Moving the rest of the team into their positions with a few hand signals, he took up his place beside the warehouse's office entrance. Holding his weapon at the ready, he counted down the breach through their links, then dropped a *go* signal at the two SWAT officers poised to punch a battering ram through the door.

Their first strike tore apart the door into a crinkled mess, catching on the penetrating end in a twist of cheap steel. Yamamoto warned for flash, then tossed three smoke grenades into the warehouse's interior, initiating a second countdown for the debilitating mist to spread through the area. Mask and protective headgear in place, Connor crossed the threshold, making the initial contact into the area and covering the doorway for the rest of the team to come through.

"Chang, inform command we're in," Connor instructed their tactical tech as the secondary team completed their breach at a similar door on the opposite end of the warehouse. "Hold fire until—"

Aware of the cops' presence, someone in the warehouse let loose with a barrage of gunfire. The sharp tap of bullets hitting the outer walls accompanied a rising flail of shouts and cries. Springing into action, Connor and Yamamoto cut through the smoke, moving quickly in a scissoring pattern to provide each other cover as they worked to cross over the warehouse's wide floor. From what Connor could see, the distribution center was mostly one long space, but stacks of boxes and abandoned air conditioning ducts deterred visibility much more than the grenades' emissions. The sleek shadows moving behind them told Connor his team was falling into position, and once Conway gave the all-clear, they moved forward to push their targets back.

Six feet in and a few turns to avoid getting tangled up in pulley chains dangling from the ceiling, the space opened up to a long bank of tables, their scarred tops littered with mounds of white crystalline shards twisted up and knotted into small sandwich bags. A larger clear package lay nearby, its top carefully split open with something sharp and its depths obviously excavated by the small coffee scoop set on a scale a few inches away.

"SFPD! Police! *Jǐngchá!*" Connor shouted out as the warehouse erupted into a wall of sound. Keeping his voice at full volume, he continued to identify them as he entered the space. "Policia! Get down! Get your head down!"

"Show us your hands." Yamamoto stepped out from behind him, keeping his attention split between the space and the corridors around them. "*Mira tus manos.* Shit, Morgan, what's that in Chinese? *Shǒu?*"

"Close," Connor replied, then repeated the direction in his fractured Cantonese. "Less people in here than I thought. Let's clear the space, and the third team can do an extraction while we go in."

The three older Hispanic women cowering under the tables kept their cries to a nearly earsplitting whine, their arms moving wildly to show their empty hands. Connor was thankful for the filtration system on his mask, but despite its steady pressure to clean the air, the faint bitter chemical tang from the open drug package floated a faint aroma across his senses.

"Down on the ground, ladies," Connor instructed as he began to pull zip ties out of a pocket on his uniform pants. "Yamamoto, catch my back as I get them secured."

"Acknowledged," his raid partner responded. "Better hurry up. I think we're going to have company."

A quick frisk of the women reassured Connor none of them had weapons, but he made hasty work of securing their limbs together, then looping ties across the table supports to prevent them from running.

Brusquely telling them to keep their heads down, Connor glanced over as Yamamoto stood at a pivot point to cover the two entry areas into the space.

"Morgan, hold down or move in?" Yamamoto's rough growl came through the link. "Never mind. They came to us."

The sound of footsteps coming toward them verified Yamamoto's prediction of company. Using a stack of dented ducts as cover, they set up in a high-low position, Yamamoto crouched at Connor's knee while Connor called to take the left. The adrenaline hitting Connor's blood was as sharp and hot as any whiskey he'd tasted, his mind going primal and focused, taking in all of the shadows and light around them.

Movement through a dark spot farther into the warehouse's cardboard warren was all the warning they had. The shadows peeled away from two desperate-looking, stringy-haired men, spitting them out in rapid succession. The one in front—a midthirties blond with scraggly hairs across his jaw line—clutched a G19 in his left hand, while the second one, a squat, flat-nosed lanky young man, waved around what looked like a SIG toward the makeshift corridor they'd come out of.

The sudden appearance of two SWAT officers was enough to startle the blond, and he swung his gun around, his fingers struggling to find the trigger. The Glock screamed, shooting a bullet off into the warehouse's ceiling, its hot brass taking flight when ejected.

"Drop your weapon and kick it to the side," Connor ordered the pair, keeping his gun level and aimed toward the older man's center mass. "Make it easy on yourselves. You don't have to go out of here in a body bag if you don't want to."

The younger man blanched to a ghostly white, then dropped his weapon, its metal housing clattering loudly on the concrete floor. Next to him, the blond glanced wildly about, as if some sort of magical exit would appear in front of him if he just looked hard enough. His companion kicking at his gun caused the older man to twirl around and fix his sights on the skinny guard's face, his Glock's muzzle trembling as his nerves kicked into overdrive.

"They're going to kill us, Scott!" Sweat beaded up on his forehead, darkening the edges of his light brown crewcut. Trapped between a pair of cops with high-powered weapons and his partner, he pleaded loudly, "Just put down your gun. I don't want to die."

Decision made, the man dropped first to his knees, then spread out quickly over the floor, stretching his limbs until his shoulder popped. With his partner grinding his nose into the warehouse's filthy concrete, the blond was forced to face the officers in front of him. When the muzzle of his gun drifted toward the tables, the women began screaming again, their terror crackling and snapping through their high-pitched screeches. Scott winced, his right shoulder rising up quickly, and he turned his body, shielding himself away from the women, but his grip on the Glock tightened.

"I don't want to hurt you, Scott." Connor eased one hand off his weapon, gesturing with his palm down and fingers spread in a slow motion toward the floor. "There's nothing in here worth you dying over. Just put the gun on the floor and step back. We'll take care of you from there. I don't want to have to tell your mom that you died over a bunch of drugs."

The blond stiffened in shock or maybe realizing Connor and Yamamoto weren't simply going to let him walk out of the place. Putting his hands over his head, Scott squatted down slowly, then placed the G19 on a piece of crumpled cardboard. His boot squelched into something wet when he stepped back, but he continued to retreat until he was standing up against a stack of boxes, giving Yamamoto enough room to kick the Glock out of reach. Connor kept his weapon trained on the men as his second-in-command secured the guards and murmured soft Irish reassurances to the women that their ordeal would be over soon.

"Area secure, Lieutenant," Chang broke through the discordance bouncing around the warehouse. "All hostiles subdued. No casualties. Opening up the channels."

The long sweet beep of an all-clear notice on the raid bounced over the comm, and Connor waited for his squad to settle down, then said, "Good job. Anyone take any damage?"

"Brad did a Conway off a docking bay, but he landed on his head, so he's good." Marshall, one of their senior team members barked a laugh.

"I swear to God, I'm going to kick every one of your asses," Conway muttered across the air.

"Chang, if you can please send in the secondaries so we can get this place cleaned up and secure," Connor ordered. "The sooner we get that done, the quicker I can send you all home."

THE AD HOC raid command center turned out to be a community center a few blocks away from the major cook site. With his team released from duty and the warehouse turned over to forensics and evidence gathering,

Connor took the initial reports they'd built out on site to be dropped off with the DA's representatives. Driving with the window down through a sleep-heavy city, he used the time to decompress after sending a text to Forest, reassuring him he was okay. As he drew closer to the operational center, traffic grew thick with official vehicles and uniformed officers. Parking his SUV as close to a checkpoint as he could, Connor flashed his credentials to get past the street-toughened sergeant tapped to keep the crowds back. She grunted an acknowledgment at Connor's star, then pointed him in the direction of where he could find coffee.

The probably bitter strong brew would keep him up all night, but Connor needed the hit. Strung out from the stress of dealing with lawyers and the court system, the drug raid seemed like a vacation, and the coffee was going to have to take the place of the margarita he might find on a sunbaked beach.

"Con!" Kane called out to him from his right. Surprised, Connor turned and waited for his younger brother to trot across the closed-off street and join him. "What are you doing here?"

"Just dropping off some paper and clearing my head before I go home." He studied his brother and tapped at the Kevlar vest covering Kane's torso. "What are you doing here? Last I heard you were still on the CAP squad. Did you get tired of the easy life and decide to join us on this side of the line?"

"Funny," Kane said flatly. "I'll remind you when you can't bend your knees anymore about how much fun you're having right now. I actually came over because one of my informants was caught up in the cook-house raid. DA was looking for someone to fill in the blanks in exchange for a deal, and my CI dropped my name."

"How much does the DA need to hear?" Connor felt a tingle of worry. "I thought everything was locked down before we went in."

"Every little bit helps," his brother pointed out. Tugging at Connor's sleeve, he nodded to a secluded corner under a closed ramen shop's awning. "Get over. I was debating whether to call you later, but apparently God wanted to spare me a dime."

It was only three, maybe four feet away, but the short distance cut the sound down around them dramatically. In the lack of pounding noise, a small headache began to throb behind Connor's left eye, and he rubbed at his brow, trying to massage loose the tight muscles across his temple.

"Johnny—my CI—has been floating around a couple of the houses, sort of picking off whatever falls to the ground, like those teeny catfish in Da's tanks." Kane nodded and smiled at a passing uniform. "Seems like the reason production kicked up over the last couple of weeks is because a few of Robinson's people didn't like the way he was working. I guess they felt like he was dragging his feet and not making as much money as he could."

"They caught Robinson in the raid?" Connor took in a quick breath. Getting a hold of the man Tate's mother put on his birth certificate had been a pipe dream since they first started to fight his removal. "Our lawyer is going to be pretty happy to get his hands on him, if they even let the firm come close. The DA is going to clamp down on Robinson pretty tight. He's not going to be able to breathe."

"That's what I'm trying to tell you. The man *isn't* breathing. Robinson's been off the board for nearly three weeks." Kane shoved his hands into his jeans, rocking back slightly. "His own guys took him out one night, and Johnny is singing every verse he knows to the DA about Robinson and a couple of other people buried in the backyard. I'm not saying that IA won't take a sniff at you, because if anybody needed Robinson gone, your name would be on that list, but the way things are looking, brother, there are at least ten other people ahead of you, and every single one of them is holding a smoking gun."

CHAPTER FIFTEEN

SITTING ACROSS the street from city hall and the Johnson Building, the squat building was an unassuming block of rectangular windows and muted gray stone. No one driving by would imagine that discussions and rulings held behind its mirrored doors could have so many consequences, but as the current seat of San Francisco's Superior and Family Courts, the shadow it cast was long and sometimes sharp.

The few times Connor had been called on to testify, he'd shown up in uniform instead of the dark gray suit he bought for a cousin's wedding. Despite knowing better, the blue tie his mother helped him knot seemed to be cutting off his air, and not even the rare sight of Forest dressed in a deep blue Mandarin collar coat and black slacks could stop the butterflies eating away at Con's stomach.

The courtroom was a subdued collection of wood paneling and beige walls. The judge's bench sat opposite the entrance, the higher seat built into a low wall of lightly stained oak that spanned the entire length of the courtroom, creating a separation between the rear door and the main space. Even though the court was freshly renovated, its patterned industrial carpet and hardback gallery chairs were chosen for durable practicality rather than to provide the room with a comfortable design.

Next to Connor, Forest shifted his weight from foot to foot, rubbing lightly at his stomach. "I shouldn't have had that coffee."

"I wish I hadn't eaten toast," Connor replied. "I thought it would help."

"I think that only helps if it's cinnamon toast." His husband leaned on Connor. "I'm just scared the judge is going to kick all of the family out. There isn't room for anybody else in here."

"Hell, I'd be better if they were on this side of the gate with us." Turning his head slightly, Connor saw his father approach behind him. "I feel like we're about to attack a Viking raiding party and I've called my entire clan to help."

"Well, ye're no wrong in that. We're right here with ye, son," his father said, squeezing Connor's shoulder with a firm grip. Donal was a massive presence behind him, as much a foundation as a cheerleader, and Connor was grateful for his father's support. "Just remember, this might be only the first step in a very long journey, but it's one we are all willing to walk with ye."

"Fortune cookies," Forest muttered under his breath. "You all sound like Irish fortune cookies."

The courtroom was filled with Morgans and musicians, outnumbering the lawyers so unevenly Connor imagined the pair of public attorneys sitting at a nearby table would feel a whole lot better if his family would stay behind the gate. With their court time slotted early in the day, Donal came dressed in his blues, prepared to go to work afterward. The rest of them were dressed in various forms of business casual, with even Miki giving a nod to the formality of the event by showing up in a leather jacket and a black button-up shirt. Kane and the twins wore their stars out, giving visual reassurance for the weapons they had on them. In the row of chairs behind them, Brigid was in a soft, murmuring conversation with Ian, who'd given Connor a tight hug when he'd come in.

"I'm going to puke," Forest whispered at Connor. "I don't have anything in my stomach except coffee, but I'm going to puke up everything I've ever eaten."

"Just don't get anything on your feet," Connor replied back. "Those are really nice boots, and I would hate to see them be ruined."

"Guys, the bailiff's about to announce the judge," their main lawyer gently informed them. "I know you are probably used to criminal court, Lieutenant, but hopefully it will be a little bit more relaxed. We'll just let the judge set the tone and go from there."

When all of the dust had settled around their case, the pack of attorneys Edie brought in plucked out a sharp-faced blond woman named Hannigan to lead the assault. Her features were all angles and hard, but she spoke with a melodic Southern accent, and from everything Connor heard, she took no prisoners.

There were more than a few times Connor was quite glad she was on his side, but scarily, Hannigan and his mother hit it off as if they were long lost cousins, leaving the Morgan family to worry about the fate of the city they lived in.

"Please remain seated. The San Francisco Unified Family Court is now in session, the Honorable Judge Meagan McNally presiding." The bailiff's deep voice rolled through the courtroom as the door behind the separation wall opened.

The judge was a bit on the short side, but she moved quickly to mount the stairs to her seat. In her midforties, she'd pulled back her wavy silver-shot auburn hair away from her face, securing it with a large-toothed clip. A bit of lace decorated the collar of her stark black robes, its pale creamy filigree providing a softening break between the solemn fabric and her plump, freckled features. Sitting down, McNally graced the courtroom with a small smile, then opened the folders the clerk had placed at her bench earlier.

"Good morning, everyone." Her voice bubbled in gentle waves, soothing and easy. "Ms. Hannigan, I have spent the last few days reading through your injunction and discussing the matter with Child Protective Services, as well as going over the supporting depositions you submitted. Before we begin, is there anything else you would like to add to my stack of paperwork here?"

"Not at this time, Your Honor," Hannigan said respectfully, rising from her chair. "As the court probably is aware, a development regarding the minor's listed paternal parent has been reported, but pending identification, we cannot enter anything formally."

"Understood." The judge turned to the pair of attorneys sitting across the aisle. "Mr. Patrick, I have it noted that you will be the representing attorney for this case, is that correct? And if so, do you have anything to add?"

The slender man who'd introduced himself earlier to Connor and Forest stood up. "Yes, Your Honor. I will be taking lead for this case. At this time, we have nothing else to introduce to the court, but we would like to reserve the right to do so if something pertinent arises."

"So noted," McNally responded. Leaning forward, she pushed up the sleeves of her robe, looking out at Connor and Forest. "First, I would like to tell you that I have spent the last hour and a half in chambers talking to the minor on record."

Connor was halfway out of his chair before he noticed he moved and realized Forest had as well. Glancing over at his husband, Connor grabbed Forest's hand, sliding their fingers together. Clearing his throat, Connor eased back down, silently entreating Forest to do the same as he spoke to the judge. "Apologies, Your Honor. The circumstances surrounding Tate's removal were... difficult."

"They wouldn't let us talk to him," Forest interjected, his voice catching as he sat. "We weren't allowed to give him any of his things. We've been worried he'd think we—"

Connor heard Forest break, then finished for him, "We didn't want him to think he'd been abandoned. Or that we didn't want him there. If we'd known he was going to be here in the building, we would've asked if we could bring him at least some clothes. Just so he had something of his own."

"I can understand and appreciate your worry, especially considering the circumstances Tate lived in prior to entering the Family Court system. And although it might not appear true, there were several people within the CPS structure who disagreed with the minor's removal." Picking up a pen, the judge rolled it between her fingers. "I will have to say that in speaking with Tate at length, I found him to be an engaging but slightly reserved young man who himself is worried... about the two of you.

"We had a long discussion about what living with you was like and how he felt about the rest of the people around you. He appreciates having a lot of uncles and aunties, especially his uncle Miki because he looks the most like Tate, but more importantly, he has a dog." The judge waited for the small rise of laughter in the courtroom to fade away before continuing. "When I initially was tagged to take up this case, I was concerned about how much time either one of you could spend with him considering your jobs, but in speaking with Tate, I learned that he's not lacking in company, either with his extended family or friends his own age.

"Some of the most poignant things I have discovered about him are the challenges he faces with food insecurity and self-esteem. He told me about the bin of canned foods under his bed and how proud he feels when he can take something from it to contribute to a meal. It is heartbreaking that this bin exists at all, but it appears to be a critical tool in Tate's emotional development." McNally's expression grew somber, but she gave them a tight smile. "I would be remiss not to recognize the solid familial foundation you can provide for him with your family, Lieutenant Morgan, but I must acknowledge how important it is that you, Mr. Ackerman, and a few of your bandmembers, have survived similar circumstances Tate has gone through. He will need compassion and empathy as he grows into himself, and it is my opinion that remaining in the foster care system will not be able to provide him that. But you can.

"I have a lot of leeway in this case, which I greatly appreciate," she continued with a tap of her pen on the desk. "Tate misses you, gentlemen, and he wants to go home. I see no reason why he shouldn't. So I am issuing a ruling that the minor in question be released back into your custody and that you may proceed to follow through on the adoption process you've already started. Officer Watson, can you please get Tate from my chambers so his fathers can take him home?"

There was more talking. Hannigan stood up again and said something that the judge responded to at length, but Connor heard none of it. There was an ache in his hand, tightening around his fingers until he realized it was Forest holding on for dear life. Neither one of them seemed to be breathing. Connor was scared to. Maybe it was lack of sleep or strung-out nerves from spending all of his energy trying to hold his life together—their lives—he had a crazy thought that if he exhaled, somehow the judge's words—the words he clung to tightly—would unravel with his breath.

The door opened and they rose as one, hands clasped together, a tremble running through Forest's arm. The bailiff swung open the tall wooden gate and an achingly familiar, beloved little boy burst through.

"Dads!" Tate was a flurry of long legs and noise, loping toward them in his awkward, slightly uncoordinated run.

It was a scramble to see who could get around the table first. There were too many chairs. Too many bodies. Too many table legs. Tate reached them before Connor resorted to picking Hannigan up and tossing her into the gallery to get her out of the way.

His mind skipped, the needle his thoughts ran along jumping merrily from one moment to the next. Scooping Tate up, Connor turned, his arms full of exuberant little boy. Then he found himself wrapped in Forest's embrace, their son between them.

"Let me look at you," Forest said. He captured Tate's chin in his hand, then let go to scrub at the boy's close-cropped black buzz cut. "What happened to your hair? Did you lose a tooth?"

"The foster lady cut it all off because lice like long hair. She cuts everybody's hair short. Even the girls." He snarled slightly, then stuck the tip of his tongue through the space in his upper teeth. "I got into a fight. One of the other guys took my shirt, and I wanted it back. It's one of my school shirts. It's at the lady's house. We'll have to get it."

"It's okay, *a mhac*," Connor reassured him, rubbing at his shoulder. While it seemed like forever since Tate had been taken, it really wasn't enough time for him to suddenly be too tall for his jeans or lose some of the baby fat in his heart-shaped face. After giving Tate a tight squeeze, he handed him over to Forest to hug. "Your hair will grow back. So will the tooth. If you never get the shirt back, it's not a big deal, okay?"

He heard Forest crying, a muted gentle sob barely audible above the chatter in the courtroom, but Connor knew every murmur and noise his husband made. Forest and their son were wrapped around each other, Tate's sneakers digging into Forest's back and his thin arms tangled as tightly around the drummer's neck as possible. Rocking Tate, Forest reassured him with soft words, promising the boy he and Connor would never let him go.

"I know, Dad," Tate croaked back, sniffling loudly. "I told them you'd come get me. They said it was bullshit, but I knew. It's okay. Don't cry."

"He's crying because he's happy, kiddo." Connor kissed the top of his son's head, then realized the judge was looking at him expectantly. Clearing his throat, he glanced around, wondering what he'd missed. "I'm sorry, Your Honor. I wasn't paying attention."

"No need to apologize, Lieutenant," Judge McNally replied, her smile broad enough to crinkle crows' feet at the corners of her eyes. "My judgment has been entered, and there have been no objections filed. Take your son home, gentlemen, and go enjoy your family."

Five Months Later

THE FIRST time Forest arrived at the Morgan family home in the Irish countryside, he'd been unsettled by the sheer amount of bright green and thundering rain, an odd reaction, he thought, considering he was born and raised in San Francisco. Still, there was something ancient stirring in the earth beneath his feet, bones of legends and battles and wild mythological tales told as history by the older members of Donal's extended family. Immersed among the Morgans, it was easy to see where Quinn got his love of beasts and supernatural ponderings. Brigid's third son often joined in when the fires were lit and whiskey was poured, the packs of children scattered about the floor in various states of half sleep, but none of them wanted to truly drop off. The stories spun invigorated the blood and sometimes stalked the edges of their nightmares, but they found it delicious fun.

Tate fit right in.

He was definitely one of the smaller kids in the pack, but he more than made up for it with his bloodlust for adventure. More than a few of Connor's elderly Irish relatives were marked with pride about how their son's fierce spirit obviously came from their side of the family. And Forest agreed. With each passing day, Tate shed more and more of his reserved nature, and two weeks deep into an immersion in the Irish countryside, he now ran wild with an underaged pack of black-haired, blue-eyed Irish marauders.

The road leading to the lake—*lough*, Forest corrected himself—was lined with old rock walls held together by moss and spackled mortar. There were breaks in the stone barrier along the way, thick copses swaying gently in the misty breeze, playing peekaboo with views of the water.

Landmarks on the lane were sparse, but Connor's directions were good enough for him to find where Con intended to take Tate and a few of his cousins fishing. A mile down the road after the orange-roofed bait shop on the pier and at the second break in the wall once he passed the red wooden chicken hammered to a stile's side post, was Old Man Corgan's pasture lands.

He heard them before he saw them—a mangled eighteen-way conversation of English and Gaelic as only five young children could hold. Forest was about to call out at the break when the trees and grasses parted.

"Forest!" Paula, a grubby female copy of her boisterous, kind mother and the de facto leader of the smaller Morgan cousins, hailed him as she fought her way out of the greenery. "Ye should have seen the fish Tam caught. It almost pulled him into the water!"

She hit the lane at a full run, the rest of her pack emerging from the weald spackled with mud and wet up to the gills. They called out to him as they got to the country road, shaking themselves off before setting off to follow Paula. When she'd gone nearly twenty yards down the road, she turned and stared back the way she came.

"Hold on!" she shouted to her familial horde. "We've got to be waiting for Tam!"

The bushes rustled again and Tate emerged from the break in the rock wall. He was as filthy, if not more than his cousins, his straight dark hair grown out long enough to get in his eyes, but the gap in his teeth was still mostly there, his incisor finally deciding to show up after a few months of coaxing. He wore Connor's old fishing shirt from a lough miles away, but from the smell of bait and other things wafting off it, it was going to take several washes before Forest could consider it clean.

"*Dia dhuit*, Dad. Da's right behind me." Tate reached out to hug Forest, then thought better of it. "I think I'm too stinky."

"I think you're right." Forest chuckled, then frowned as a small, potbellied black terrier ambled out onto the road, its stubby legs working hard to catch up with the little boy he was following. "What the hell? Where did that come from?"

"Oh, he's decided I'm his," his son replied casually, stretching his arms out to shake as much of the mud off his hands as possible without getting any on Forest. "Moira from the bait shop said he's been waiting for me going on a couple of days now, but Paula thinks someone put him in a bag and threw him into the lake and Moira found him. She says assholes do that sometimes, but we're not to call Moira a liar because if that's what she wants to think, that's okay."

"I see ye met our son's new friend." Unlike the children, Connor was nearly silent as he came onto the road. Much cleaner but not that much drier than the pack of chattering kids standing a ways down the road, he carried a handful of fishing poles and a small cooler. "Tate, ye go on with yer kin. Yer dad and I will be down by the house. We'll take the puppy with us."

Forest scooped up the scruffy small dog before he could run after Tate when the boy took off after his cousins. Shouting after his son, he asked, "Did he at least tell you his name?"

Tate spun around in midleap, yelling back, "It's Gaige!"

Sighing heavily, Forest tilted his head up to drink in the soft kiss Connor offered him. The puppy wiggled, trying to get loose, but Forest held on. The terrier let out a few scolding barks, then huffed, resigned to his prison.

Forest sorted through all of the questions popping up in his brain. They had a mile walk back to the sprawling house the Morgans owned, and the day was nice enough, although he knew Ireland's weather well enough to know it could go sharp and wet within moments of saying the sun was out. He had more than enough time to shake out all the answers he needed from Connor along the way.

Choosing one, he asked, "Why are they calling him Tam?"

"Tate Ackerman Morgan," Connor explained. "So, Tam it was. Then came the long argument about Tam Lin and Irish folklore, so I told them to hound Quinn about it. He'll be setting them straight on that. I wasn't going to go down that rabbit hole with that bunch."

"How are we going to get a dog home?" Forest examined the puppy's cute face. He loved how Connor's accent deepened the longer they spent in Ireland, but he was well aware of his weakness for the Emerald Isle lilt in his husband's voice. "Even better, where did it—he—come from, and how the hell did the kid talk you into taking him home?"

"Well, we stopped for bait and snacks. Mostly snacks, to be honest, because I didn't think fishing was going to hold their attention for too long. Moira was telling me about how she'd gaffed a trash bag out of the water, and well then, there it was. She's been caring for it this past week now, but she's already got three of her own. So Tate was sitting on the steps, and the puppy literally tumbled into his lap." Connor shrugged, giving Forest a wicked smile. "It took a liking to him. Or rather, he took a liking to him. We'll figure it out. Come on. Let's go home so I can lie about how big of a fish I had to toss back."

Forest cradled the terrier against him, then sniffed at Connor when his husband looped an arm over Forest's shoulders.

"I didn't get anything on me but water," Connor teased. "The children were the ones who seem to have problems staying on shore. I spent more time dragging them out of the water than I did fishing. And it will be fine, *a ghra*. Ye'll see. With any luck we'll have the wee thing housebroken before we get home."

"Great." Forest ducked his head to the side as the puppy tried to nip at his nose. "Gaige, huh? I'm assuming that's Irish."

Connor's laugh caught the attention of the dog, who tried to stretch his body to lick at Connor's face. "It is *definitely* Irish."

The terrier was stubborn, determined to get its way, and it became a struggle of wills for Forest to hold on to him. Amused, Forest asked, "So what does Gaige mean?"

Connor stopped in the middle of the road, took the wildly squirming puppy out of Forest's arms, and handed him the fishing rods to carry home. Smiling, Forest's Irish cop gave him a quick kiss, then murmured, "It means Dude."

Keep Reading for an Excerpt from
Fish Stick Fridays
by Rhys Ford

PROLOGUE

DEACON REID and the dark were old friends.

He'd grown up in the shadows, suckling on the comfort and safety they gave him. It was when he was dragged out into the open—that was when trouble started. Light threw the world into a tizzy for Deacon. It was too unyielding, too raw in its truth. He couldn't hide away the things he didn't want to know about himself if he stood too long in the light of day, especially once he'd grown big enough to hurt others before they could hurt him.

So why he was sleeping with a night-light on, Deacon Reid had no fricking clue.

Then a tiny poodle snore from the motel bed next to his kicked it all back into perspective.

He was no longer alone, no longer able to hide in the shadows of society with one eye on the game and the other watching for the law. Deacon'd been brought down by the one thing he thought he'd never in his life ever have—a little girl.

The night-light was nonnegotiable. It was the one thing Zig's foster mother'd packed up along with the few pieces of clothing that still fit her. From his own experience in the system, Deacon figured it was less about fit and more about what she'd been able to hang on to. Nothing lasted forever in foster care or juvie. He'd been lucky to hold on to a few pairs of underwear the first few months he'd been passed around. Zig hadn't been as fortunate.

Stealing Deacon's things was a guaranteed right hook to the offender. His young niece probably didn't pack the same kind of punch. Of course, he'd gone into juvie as a nearly six-foot-tall thirteen-year-old with a two-by-four on his shoulder, while Zig was an eight-year-old little girl who needed a night-light to keep the monsters at bay when she slept.

Deacon knew all about monsters.

He'd nearly devoted his entire life to becoming one.

Zig's snore went from cute fluttery noises to full-out audio warfare, and Deacon briefly debated the pros and cons of putting a pillow over her head just long enough for him to get some sleep. Since CPS tended to frown on things like that, he resigned himself to getting out of bed and getting something cold out of the cooler he'd dragged in from his truck.

A four-in-the-morning beer was out of the question. Hell, packing any beer in the cooler wasn't even on the think about list. He had to watch everything he did, everyone he spoke to. One misstep, and Zig would be right back where she'd started before a skeptical judge'd given him custody—caught in the quagmire of foster homes and overstressed CPS workers. Not what he wanted for his baby sister's little girl, not by a long shot.

The room's rubber-backed curtains were old-school, thick, and heavy enough to kick back any ambient light coming from the highway rest stop attached to the motel, but Zig's little plug-in teddy bear spat out more than enough glow to see by. Still, Deacon didn't spot one of her boots until he was nearly right on top of it. Stepping quickly to avoid tumbling over it, he swung his foot around and smacked his toes into Zig's metal bedframe.

"Fuck." Deacon caught his tongue between his teeth and bit down before he could say any more. He held his breath, waiting to see if Zig would wake up, but a too long second later, another sputtering, feathery snore came from the lump under the bed linens.

Nothing. No movement. Not a snuffle. He was safe… with a slick of blood-tinged spit over his tongue, but still… safe.

He'd been warned. Every single Child Protective Services person he ran up against warned him off of Zig, more for Zig's sake than his, but Deacon'd been determined. He was going to raise Deanna's little girl for her. It was the least he could do, considering he hadn't been around when she'd needed him the most.

Now he was left with a shattered eight-year-old with a stubborn love of pink tutus and combat boots who'd had to wash her mother's dried blood and brains off of her feet before she called the cops.

Still, Deacon thought as he stared down into the cooler's selection of drink packets and Ziploc bags of string cheese and cut-up vegetables, a beer still would have been nice.

The drive up from Chula Vista to Northern California took longer than he'd wanted—nearly three days instead of the straight hard push through on one try. Traveling with little girls was problematic, especially with Zig's tiny bladder. When she'd seen a sign pointing the way to Disneyland, Deacon'd given up any pretense they were going to make it into Half Moon Bay before Saturday.

It took a few hundred dollars, a hell of a lot of sugar, and one squishable blue alien plushie before Zig willingly said adios to the Land of the Mouse and they'd gone on their way.

On the plus side of things, the Main Street candy shop had a clearance sale, and he'd scored a few pounds of lemon drops, his answer to nicotine gum to help kick smoking.

"Fruit punch kind of goes with lemon drops," he muttered, peering through the darkness in the hopes he could pick out the one he wanted. There were flavor traps smuggled into juice packs, most notably a spinach-hued concoction heralding the return of the Green Gooberry. It was like sucking on a piece of broccoli's armpits and apparently one of Zig's favorites. Fishing out a juice, he shook off the excess water, then carefully closed the cooler. "She's fucking welcome to them."

Something made Deacon straighten up and take notice, an imperceptible wrongness hovering about the room. Something… changed.

There was a filth to the air, a shifting scent he couldn't quite pinpoint. Standing as still as he could in the middle of the motel room, Deacon closed his eyes and listened, absorbing the world as it moved around him.

Something definitely changed.

A crackle tickled his senses, barely audible over Zig's tiny snores and the periodic thundering of a semi barreling past on the highway a few yards away. The tickle grew stronger, languidly slapping at his brain, then coyly slipped away. Something darker joined it. A touch of waste reached him, a curled stink hooking up into his sinuses and burning its way down to his belly. There was a touch of diesel in the air, typical for all engines loading up nearby, but it was something deeper—something more primal—a fear Deacon couldn't shake.

The tickle turned, going dark and sooty. Then something behind the motel burst—and the world caught on fire.

Flames chewed through the long wall across of the beds, a hot trail of sparks and popping sounds scrambling across the room's faded wallpaper. Ash swirled on the fire-spin breeze being kicked up as the motel's baked-sun wooden frame struggled to stay fixed to its cinder-block base.

"Zig! Get up!" There were no smoke alarms. There should have been alarms, but Deacon heard nothing, saw nothing other than the plumes of smoke beginning to fill the room. Zig's shoes went onto the bed next to her. Then his duffel bag joined them as she lifted her head from the pillow, her tangled mass of brown curls erupting into a ball around her pinched-in face.

"What? Uncle Deke, what?" Her voice, plaintive and scratchy, sounded like her mother's had when Deanna was her age. She was a restless sleeper, yanking all of the linens up from under the mattress until she'd built herself a little nest. A cough shook her tiny body, then another. "I'm tired—"

"Fuck it. Grab on to me, kiddo." Deacon scooped the fitted sheet from the bed, pulling up the ends until he rolled Zig and their things into a bundle. He felt her little arms close around his neck, and he lifted everything up, holding on tight.

The smoke thickened, burning Deacon's eyes. He blinked away a wash of tears, realizing he couldn't see the door anymore. Moving mostly by feel, he walked until he hit a wall. Zig's coughing grew worse, and his own lungs were beginning to burn. A brush of a curtain on his arm startled him, but Deacon edged along the wall, keeping his bare toes on the edge of the carpet until he felt the sharp sting of the door's metal and rubber draft catcher digging into his foot.

Zig's body convulsed in his embrace as her coughing began in earnest, and Deacon raced to find the doorknob while keeping a tight grip on his niece. A frantic handful of moments later, his grasping fingers found their target, and he turned the knob—only for the door to catch on the triangular hook latch he'd thrown over its ball to prevent anyone from coming in.

"Can you grab that, baby girl?" Deacon rasped, catching a lungful of cool air coming in from the partially opened door. Zig bent forward, nearly toppling them both over, but she grabbed at the latch, flinging it back while Deacon canted the door just enough for it to be released.

"There!" Zig fell into another bout of coughing, twisting as Deacon shouldered his way past the open door and into the diesel-scented air outside. He'd gotten nearly halfway across the truck lot toward where he'd parked his old Chevy and the enclosed half-bed trailer he'd towed his Harley in when Zig screamed, "My night-light!"

FISH STICK FRIDAYS

"Screw it. I'll buy you—" The ground shook under Deacon's feet. Then a hot blast of wind lifted them both up, carrying Deacon forward. A hiccup-moment later, a boom rumbled over them, swaddling any other sounds. Deacon's ears popped from the force of the blast, and his stomach lurched as he twisted in midair, trying to cradle Zig and everything else he was carrying against him.

He landed hard, skipping across the asphalt on his back, a soft stone on a tarry, hard lake. His shirt gave, and underneath it, so did his skin, but Deacon held on tight, gritting his teeth against the pain. He bounced one last time, nearly ten feet away from where his truck sat among a few semis and RVs. Smoke coated the sky's belly, blocking out even the ambient light coming from a gas station across the road. There were shouts, fading into the distance and nearly buried in the swooshing sound running through his ears.

Zig's frightened crying, however, drowned out even his fear.

"Hey, Zig. It's all good. We're fine." Sitting up was hard. He ached, and Deacon was sure he'd left most of his skin on the parking lot. Shuffling Zig around in his arms, he uncovered her soot-grimed face from the sheet wrapped over it. His duffel with their clothes and things fell out of the makeshift pouch, landing at Zig's bare feet.

Shifting around, Deacon stared through Zig's tangled mass of curls at the burning motel. The blast'd thrown them several yards, well past the debris field kicked up by whatever blew them sky high. Cinder block chunks lay a few feet away from where Deacon and Zig sat, deadly projectiles they'd not have survived if one'd hit. The bones of several rooms were scattered about, smoldering wood chunks and broken furniture thrown wide and far. Someone nearby was screaming, pleading with God and whoever else was listening to come help her husband.

Fishing his keys out of his bag with one hand, Deacon rocked Zig as her sobs lessened. Standing was harder than sitting up, but Deacon forced himself onto his feet. Once he got the Chevy's passenger door unlocked, he sat Zig down on the seat. His ears popped again, and the world flooded back into full volume, carrying sirens and shouts to his rattled brain.

"Stay here, Zig," Deacon ordered. "I'm going to go help that woman. Okay? Do not move."

She nodded, her tearstained face glistening in the smoke-rippled light. Clutching her plush doll tightly, Zig stared back at the room where they'd been sleeping. "Uncle Deke?"

Zig never called him uncle, yet twice tonight, she'd slipped that endearment in. Deacon glanced over his shoulder at where the woman sat on the lot, her hands pressing down on her too still husband's body, trying to hold back the blood gushing out of his naked back.

"I gotta go, kiddo. I'll be right back," he promised. "Don't let anyone touch you. I'll be right over there."

"Be careful, Deke," Zig warned, hiccupping through her halting sobs. "I think someone don't like us."

CHAPTER ONE

"THIS PLACE looks like shit," Zig proclaimed as she climbed out of Deacon's old Chevy. Scanning the sign hanging above one of the shop's open bay doors, she wrinkled her nose at her uncle, craning her neck back to further smear her disgust into his face. "Who the hell is Artie?"

"He's the guy I bought the place from." Slapping a bit of road dust from his jeans, Deacon took a long, hard look at the place he'd dumped all of his money into.

He just wasn't sure it was worth it.

Getting custody of Zig meant losing everything he had. With a misdemeanor prison stint hanging over his head and an iffy career at building custom bikes, Child Protective Services and the Family Court definitely hadn't bent over backward to give him the kid. It'd taken nearly eight months of wrangling, pleading, and rearranging his life back in Atlanta before someone finally decided to give Zig over.

Now Deacon wondered if that someone hadn't been insane.

Most of his belongings—anything worth anything—had been sold off, leaving him with the battered truck, his Harley Road King, and a recently acquired matching sidecar he'd picked up in a swap for a 351 Windsor. The Harley and sidecar sat in a trailer behind the truck with its ugly white shell meant to keep the elements off of the cardboard boxes he and Zig'd stuffed their lives into.

All he had left so he could be the sole owner of Artie's Motors, a mechanic's shop in a California coast town called Half Moon Bay.

From the looks of the peeling gray-blue paint on the last wooden structure on one of the town's historical downtown strips, Artie's Motors had seen better days to say the least. To say the worst—it looked like the shit Zig'd declared it to be.

"And it's not shit. It's crap. Language, Zig." He remembered at the last minute. She was already a few feet away from the truck, stomping through a puddle and getting mud on the pair of cheap black pleather boots he'd bought from a swap meet. "You can't say shit anymore."

"You say it."

She stopped, her shoulders back and spine straightened. Despite her light caramel coloring and saffron-blonde curly mane, there was no denying they were related. He'd felt himself give others the exact same look she was giving him, a mental fuck you layered with a middle finger against authority.

A definite promise that the next decade was going to be fucking hell if she had anything to say about it.

"Yeah, best part about being an adult," he countered, "is that I'm the one who gets to use adult words. Not yours."

"When?" The challenge was still there, hidden beneath the crafty tilt of her soft voice.

"When what?"

"When do I get to use them? The adult words." Zig cocked her head at him, another gesture they either shared or she'd picked up from him. "And can you make a list? You know, so I don't forget what they are."

"When you're sixteen. You can say shit then, and you'll remember. I'll tell you once to not say something." Deacon returned her fake, patient smile. "After that, money comes out of your stash and into the half-assed jar." He raised his hand, cutting her off as she opened her mouth. "No arguing this one. CPS will have my fucking head if you spit bad words at your grandmother when they take you to visit."

"I wouldn't say them to her." Zig snorted delicately as she continued to stomp through the water pools at the shop's main door. "She'd shit a pig."

"Quarter a word, kid." He poked a finger at her shoulder when he walked by. "It'll add up fast so... choose wisely."

"Well, fuck." He heard her mutter at his back, but Deacon let that one ride.

He was too overwhelmed by the stark reality of owning an auto shop that might have been better off being burned to the ground for the insurance money.

FISH STICK FRIDAYS

Artie's seemed like a good deal—nearly too good—but the business checked out. It had a good reputation, the books were solid, and it came with two long-time employees whose salary was supported by the work the shop brought in.

It was the outside that made Deacon pull up short and wonder what the hell Artie'd spent his money on.

Sitting at the short end of an L, the shop was nearly as deep as it was wide, a three-bay wooden structure with cracked paint and grease-smeared windows. Situated at the end of a cul-de-sac, the shop was connected on the left by a string of other businesses, all geared more for Half Moon Bay's upper-class leisurely lifestyle than Artie's. It was a downtown with cheese shops, artisanal bakeries, cupcake stores, and a couple of microbreweries, definitely more hip than the run-down SoCal industrial park he'd worked in last. Cobblestone walks and old trees lining the streets, Half Moon Bay looked more like a set from a 1950s television show than a place to live.

From what Deacon could see, the diagonal parking along the broad street seemed ample enough, and the shop had an asphalt slab to the right and stretching out around to the back of the property, allowing for vehicle storage if he needed it. At least he hoped business would be good enough he'd need that much space. If not, he didn't know what he and Zig were going to do.

Part of a longer building, the auto shop shared a wall with a hair salon. The rest of the businesses were sturdy ones: a dance studio, another of those cheese shops he'd seen, and a bookstore that took up at least as much room as the other three shops next to it. Artie's was the only one without a covered walkway but did at least have an awning protecting the front door.

From the looks of the water puddles on the ground and the lush green space running down the right side of the cul-de-sac, Half Moon Bay seemed to get a lot of rain.

"Seriously, crap." Zig sniffed at her hands. "And I still smell, Uncle Deke. We're going to have to wash Stitch. He smells too."

"Soon as we go find the house. There's a washing machine there. Everything in the bag's gotta go in. Maybe you too. Shit, hope the place doesn't leak." Deacon stared up at the store's tall parapet. He couldn't see the roof beyond the old-fashioned wooden front, but if it was as neglected as the exterior, he'd have to see about waterproofing the shop as soon as he could. He could have sworn he heard his wallet whimpering from his back pocket.

"I've got to go piss," she declared loudly, startling a woman coming out of the salon. "Can we go inside so I can use the bathroom?"

Zig was beginning to do the dancing shuffle she did when a potty break was imminent, and any doubt about his niece's bladder were put to rest when she bounced on the balls of her feet. She'd dressed herself that morning, donning a pink tutu, green camo T-shirt, and her thick black boots. As usual, her hair was a puffball of gold and brown curls, and they'd fought a bit to get it brushed, then contained in a scrunchie. From the looks of things, her hair'd definitely won that battle, because the scrunchie was nowhere to be seen.

"Yeah, hold your horses, kid." One of the bay doors was partially open, a few inches off of the ground, and he'd seen movement inside of the front office, a blur behind the smudged, grimy glass. "I've got to go check it out."

Deacon was cautious, wary even, but finding the front door unlocked worried him more than he'd like to admit. He became less worried when a tall, skinny man with thin blond hair wearing an Artie's Motors work shirt stepped into the office from a door leading to the work bays, his sharp chin up in a slight challenge.

"Can I help you? We're closing up for the day, but I can see what we can do for you tomorrow."

His embroidered name tag said Eli, but Deacon couldn't imagine a less likely name for the lanky mechanic. He looked more like a cartoon character, all elbows and knocking knees with a jut of an Adam's apple nearly as pushed out as his chin.

"Half day on Sundays, you know?"

"Hey, um… Eli?" Deacon held his hand out to the younger man. If Eli was twenty-five, Deacon'd be surprised. "Deacon. Deacon Reid. I'm the new owner."

"Can you hurry it up, babe? I want to catch—"

Deacon doubted most mechanics called one another babe unless done sarcastically, but from the shocked, slightly frightened look on the short, barrel-chested man's face, he guessed Abe—or so his name tag said—meant it in the most endearing of ways.

"Shit. Um—"

FISH STICK FRIDAYS

"This is Mr. Reid. He's the new owner." Eli practically stabbed Abe with the pointed gaze he gave him. Turning back to Deacon, he smiled weakly, the corners of his thin mouth wavering. "Sorry. We weren't expecting you until tomorrow."

Deacon could feel the fear rolling off of the young men. It stung the air, wrapping around them both in a choking terror. Abe trembled, seemingly wanting to flee but man enough to put himself between Deacon and Eli. He caught their hands touching, the briefest of touches but tender despite the scrape of their work-roughened fingers.

Abe cleared his throat as he hitched his pants up by the belt loops. "Look, if you've got a problem—"

"It's all good, but let's get one thing out of the way, okay?" Deacon'd have to kill the pink elephant standing in the middle of the room, so he nodded once at Abe and Eli. The other mechanic blanched to a light gray under his heavy five o'clock shadow. "You're gay, right? Together?"

They made noises, sad, fumbling noises. Then Abe ran his hands through his thick black hair, making it stand up on end. "Um... shit. We—"

"Look. I like dick and ass as much as the next guy. Seeing as you two are the next guy, I'm guessing a lot. One rule, no fucking around in the place. I'd say the same to anyone, straight or not. I've got a niece. She's eight. She's going to learn about the birds and the bees when I tell her about them." Deacon jerked his thumb back toward where Zig stood bouncing on the sidewalk. "I'm not going to be hanging a rainbow flag out or anything, but I don't care if you kiss in front of the customers, and if anyone gives you shit, they're out of here. Got it?"

"Mr. Reid—"

"It's Deacon. And that's a yes or no question."

"Yeah, okay," Eli responded quickly. "We're good with that."

They nodded together, their heads bobbing in unison, and Deacon continued, "Mostly we're not hanging a flag 'cause I don't have a rainbow flag, but—"

"Deke! I've gotta take a piss!" Zig screamed at him, pressing her face into the window until her nose was pushed up into a piggy snout. "Or I'm gonna pee on the sidewalk! Do you want CPS to know I'm peeing on the sidewalk? Can you hear me, Deke?"

"And that's Zig. Get in here!" Deacon tapped at the glass, motioning toward the partially open door. Glancing back at the still quivering Eli, he asked. "Where's the bathroom?"

"Over there. That door." Eli pointed at one of the two doors on the long wall behind the office's reception counter. Zig rushed past them, and Abe let out a small grunt, bumping into the wall to avoid being hit. "The other one's the office, but it's kind of a mess. We try keeping up the work area, but in here was all Artie's."

As shops went, it wasn't really that bad. Especially when Deacon took into account the outside.

The walls needed painting, preferably after a hard scrubbing with vinegar and water, because Artie or his crew smoked like chimneys, something Deacon was going to have to bring to a stop. But neither man smelled like ash, so he was going to lay the stench right at Artie's feet. A lingering reek of cheap tobacco clung to the air, and Deacon scraped his tongue against his teeth to get rid of its taste in his mouth. A wide door connected the front office to the bays, and peering through the opening, he was pleasantly surprised at its cleanliness. Whatever neglect the front suffered, the work areas seemed to have escaped a similar dire fate.

"The toilet's broken." Zig stomped out. "It keeps making water. And I had to hover because there's oil on the seat. It's disgusting."

"Yeah, the handle needs replacing, but Artie said the new owner could deal—um, he figured you'd take care of that." Eli shifted toward Abe, placing himself a little bit behind the shorter, muscular man.

"Probably need to jiggle the handle," Deacon replied absently. "Go back in and do that, Zig. Then wash your hands."

A good scrubbing, and the front office would be as good as new, or at least as good as he could make it. The business'd come up for sale under the premise of Artie retiring, but now Deacon wondered if the place'd grown to be too much to maintain. A quick peek into the work office confirmed his suspicions. There looked to be two desks in the room and two windows, one looking out into the lot behind the shop and the other into the work bays. Paper littered nearly every flat surface, and a file cabinet was stuffed to the brim, its drawers partially open and bristling with colored folders.

FISH STICK FRIDAYS

"Yeah, Artie kind of just tossed stuff in there." Abe chimed in, his voice dropping an octave when Deacon winced at the office. "We'll help you go through it if you want."

"That'll be cool. I'll need help knowing what to toss." Deacon caught Eli's Adam's apple bobble. "If you guys want to head out, go ahead. I just came by to take a look around. Sounds like you've got plans, and we've still got to go find our house."

"You don't mind?" Abe rumbled. "I mean, we can stick around if you're thinking about cleaning up some of Artie's stuff. We just didn't want to touch it because—"

"He was particular," Eli finished. "Just told us we had to hang in here until you got in." They exchanged a look. Then Abe nodded. "Wasn't sure if you'd want us to still work here or if you were going to bring in your own guys."

"Hey, the bays are clean from what I can see, and Artie's shitty about housekeeping, but his books were solid. I'm not planning on changing anything except maybe the paint outside, cleaning up in here, and changing the place's name." Deacon knocked on the bathroom door. "You drowning in there, Zig?"

"The faucet handle came off. I got the water to stop, though. There's a switch thing under the sink." Zig came back out again, her hands dripping water onto the office's scuffed-up linoleum floor.

"Okay, and fixing the sink," he added, smiling back when Eli's grin grew wide enough to nearly reach his ears. "And nah, go on and lock up. We can start tomorrow."

Zig kicked at the pressboard wall of the counter, denting its vinyl side. "Sh—oops. Sorry. Hey, Deke, do I have to go to school tomorrow? Or what?"

"Probably or what. Don't worry about the counter. It's going to come out." A calendar on the wall behind the front desk was either selling breast enlargements or motor oil, depending on how he interpreted its offer to be tuned up. The dates were off, but then the calendar was also from three years ago, so it had that going for it. Probably Artie's contribution to the décor. "Today's Sunday. The school needs some paperwork and shit—stuff—done before they'll let you in. But probably sometime this week."

"Great." She slumped down into the office chair behind the desk, yelping when it almost tipped over backward. "Shit! Fuck."

"I'll give you that one for free." Deacon grinned down at her. "Now, how about if we go grab some food and go find that house we've got rented. I'm ready to go home."

Sundays At Between the Lines Bookstore were always sparsely attended. The fog rolled out early that morning and stayed, leaving a chill in the air cold enough to warrant a roaring fire in the store's old river-stone fireplace and a pot of hot drinking chocolate for customers. In fact, if Lang really was honest with himself, he would have used the word dead, but as the store's owner, he liked to keep a sheen of delusion over the whole matter.

Especially since it meant he could spend a quiet Sunday afternoon sitting in a leather armchair, sipping hot chocolate in front of the store's fireplace. A far better afternoon than going through his dead grandmother's belongings.

So far his quiet day only had one loud wrinkle in it—Yvonne Dupree, who Lang swore could smell him opening a bag of chocolate chips from a mile away. Her own shop, Shear Perfection, also took a hit from the weather, as nearly all of their Sunday appointments rescheduled, leaving a single weave job for Yvonne to do, and she'd been looking for something sweet before spending a few hours chatting up her customer.

Still, the sturdy black woman was good company, entertaining and sweet despite of or perhaps because of her running commentary on the people wandering about their little street. One thing was for certain, Yvonne definitely brought a little bit of much-needed zest into Lang's staid life. She'd grabbed a stoneware mug, filled it with hot chocolate, then critiqued Lang's shaggy, unkempt hair for about five minutes while he nodded in silent agreement. Yvonne left in as much of a storm as the clouds hammering down on them, taking most of the wind with her but leaving a sizzling spark of a kiss on Lang's cheek.

"Close up early and come down to get that mane of yours cut, boy," she'd scolded from the bookstore's entrance. "You look like one of those sheepdogs that boy at the coffee shop owns."

It'd been a thought. A very quick fleeting thought before he dug out an old copy of Gossamer Axe from his book bag and plopped down

FISH STICK FRIDAYS

into one of the reading nooks. He'd left the shop's french doors partially open, more to hear the incoming rain than to welcome any roaming, storm-fearing customers.

There'd been little action along their short street, with the exception of an old red truck pulling a trailer behind it. The same beaten-up red truck that came to a shuddering stop on its way out of the cul-de-sac— right in front of Between the Lines bookstore, and Lang heard a little girl yelling at the top of her lungs.

"A bookstore! Stop, Deke, books!" The screeching dropped to a loud growl. "Deke! Come on!"

From the deeper rumble of a man's voice, Lang had a good idea he was going to get a couple of customers whether he wanted them or not. Sticking a piece of tattered lace in his book to mark his place, Lang leaned over to warn off the twenty-pound marmalade cat curled up in the next chair, tapping the dozing feline on the nose.

"No biting anyone, Fafhrd. Only reason I brought you in today was because it's usually dead." Lang quickly glanced out the windows, resigned to the interruption to his Sunday. The cat he'd inherited from his grandmother opened one baleful golden eye, then closed it again, leaving a sneer behind. Sighing, Lang scritched the cat's head, then stood up as the cat gave him a disgruntled mew. "Great. Good to know you're with me on this."

The little girl hit first, a whirlwind of hair, dirty pink tutu, and thick-soled black boots. She was a wild child, an urban street waif with cunning green eyes and honey-toned skin, confident and strong as she strode through the shop's doors. Lang was about to ask her if she needed any help, but she met his gaze briefly, then dismissed him, as neatly done as Lang's mother waved off a waiter. Stomping past the sweeping antique reception sectional Lang used as a checkout counter, the wee termagant headed straight into the fiction stacks without tossing a single glance behind her.

Following her seemed like a good idea, if only to help her get a book down from one of the taller shelves, when a man Lang could only assume was the infamous truck-driving Deke came in, and Lang lost any grasp of language he might have woken up with. Possibly even all he'd ever learned, because Deke's powerful body shoved everything aside.

By everything Lang held holy and dear, the sight of the little girl's Deke nearly brought him to his knees.

There was something about a rough-around-the-edges man that did Lang in. It might have been his own silver-spoon upbringing and years of private school, where knowing what fork to use was as important as mastering algebra, but whatever it was, the man he suspected was Deke pushed every single one of his on buttons.

Deke was tall, built lean, with rippling muscles keenly outlined by the tight fit of a wash-worn blue T-shirt stretched over his shoulders and broad back. His torso narrowed into a trim waist, a pair of equally worn jeans riding low over his hips and held up by a firm rounded ass. Deke's razor hadn't touched his face for several days at least, judging by the scruff over his jaw and upper lip, and his golden-brown hair lay in a mess around his face, windblown or finger combed with a carelessness Lang could only envy. He had the same Aegean-Sea-green eyes as the little girl, and filled with about as much masculine presence and wariness as they could hold.

Lang couldn't remember the last time he'd found another man attractive. There'd been trips into Half Moon Bay with friends, mostly for dancing and, once in a great while, a quick mutual hand job in the bathroom of a club, but nothing resembling a relationship.

Not since Daniel—and the less he thought of that fiasco, the better.

Fafhrd wasn't as tongue-tied. The hefty cat slithered off of his chair and slunk over to the man's ankles before Lang could catch him. He took a step forward, his breath caught behind clenched teeth as the little girl's Deke bent down to greet the cat.

"Hey, who's this?"

There was always a moment when the marmalade cat decided if he liked someone or not, and Lang only exhaled when Fafhrd nudged the man's knee and mewled sweetly to be scratched.

"That's Fafhrd," Lang offered up, unreasonably envious of the cat's massage.

"Yeah?"

Deke's green eyes pierced through Lang, leaving him stumbling over his own teeth.

"Where's the Gray Mouser?"

In that second, Lang was fairly certain he'd fallen halfway in love. Or would have if his first customer of the day hadn't come stomping back with her arms laden with two heavy books. Plopping them up on the counter, she looked expectantly at Deke. Disturbed by the boot clomps, Fafhrd stalked back to his chair, his tail lifted behind him in an arrogant salute.

"These are the ones I want, Uncle Deke." She ran her hand over the top book. "I think I have enough."

"Funny how you only call me uncle when you want something." Lang's wet dream strolled over to the counter, dwarfing his niece. "Let's see what you've got."

They were popular books, a boy wizard's battle against forces of evil, and Lang had to fight to hide a grin as the child began to explain away her choices. Her uncle listened carefully, most of his attention on his niece, but at one point of the story, he looked up and caught Lang's eye.

And winked.

Lang felt that wink down to his balls.

"Might be above her reading level," Lang heard himself saying.

He got two looks—bemused from the uncle and a look of horrified disgust from the little girl.

"She reads above her height," Deke replied. "Sometimes too damned high, but we're working on that."

"I've got the whole series in a packaged set. Comes in a cardboard chest." He got his bearings, finding the floor beneath his feet again until the girl turned to eye him suspiciously. "It's cheaper that way. Per book anyway. They're over here."

The girl was gone and back before Lang could offer to fetch her one. Sniffing loudly, her face fell when she found the box's price tag.

"I don't have this much. Shit."

"Got less now, Zig," Deke drawled. "Quarter gone."

"Fu—this sucks." Zig's hair bobbed about her head as she moved. "Can I get an advance?"

Her uncle broke into a grin. "Nope. No loans. You know why."

"'Cause interest means you're paying more than something's worth." She glanced at the two tomes she'd already pulled down from the shelves. "I've already read the first one, but I want the whole thing."

"Tell you what. I'll buy the set, and when you've earned the money, you can buy the other books off of me." Deke turned the case over. "So it's fifty-two bucks for these. What's that come out to?"

"Seven-something dollars a book," she crowed, then waved her hands about. "No—fuck. Taxes. Okay, wait. I can do this."

"She's antigovernment right now. Thinks it's unfair hot food gets taxed at the grocery store. Mostly because she really likes buying those deli chickens for dinner."

The man smelled of lemons and lightning with a dash of rain, and as Deke whispered over the counter, Lang felt Deke's breath rush warm over his cheek.

"Lost another quarter there, Zig."

"Eight something. 'Cause the tax is almost five bucks on the whole thing. Right?"

"About four. So yeah, eight bucks a book." Deke hefted the case in his large hand. "Sure you want it? Can you make the loan?"

"Easy." She made a face. "If I don't swear."

"Yeah, that's killing you." Her uncle handed the books over to Lang. "Wrap 'em up. Oh, and Zig, no breaking into them until we get the truck unpacked."

"It's raining!"

Her protest rattled Fafhrd, who meowed loudly back.

"There's a garage. Or so I've been told. The bike can stay in the trailer, but the rest of it's got to go into the house." Deke had his wallet on the counter, pulling out his bank card. Muttering under his breath, he shook his head at Lang. "As soon as I find the damned house."

They were gone nearly as soon as Lang handed Zig the bag. She gave him a curt nod, then was out of the shop, almost hitting Yvonne on her way out. Deke—Deacon—was slower, pausing long enough to hold the door open for the woman, calling her ma'am before he jogged through the rain to get to the truck. Yvonne stood watching them both for a minute, then came inside, fanning herself dramatically with one hand.

"Damn, that boy could make an ice cube sizzle." Sidestepping around a prowling Fafhrd, Yvonne headed to the pot of simmering hot chocolate. "That girl, though. Someone needs to show him how to handle our kind of hair."

"You probably can bring it up to him. He bought Artie's shop. That's Deacon Reid." Lang wiped his hands on his jeans, marveling at how damp his palms were. "But then, he might not like unsolicited advice."

FISH STICK FRIDAYS

"Hey, if he cleans up the outside of that place, I'll do the girl's hair for free for as long as he owns it," Yvonne declared loudly, nudging Fafhrd out of her way with her foot. "'Course judging by the way he took that one last look of you before he left, I'm guessing the building isn't the only thing that boy wants to paint."

RHYS FORD is an award-winning author with several long-running LGBT+ mystery, thriller, paranormal, and urban fantasy series; a two-time LAMBDA finalist; and a multiple Gold and Silver Medalist by the Florida Authors and Publishers President's Book Awards. She is published by Dreamspinner Press, DSP Publications, and Rogue Firebird Press.

She shares the house with Harley, a gray tuxedo with a flower on her face, Badger, a disgruntled former alley cat, and Gojira, a mercurial Tabico. She is also enslaved to the upkeep of a 1979 Pontiac Firebird named Tengu and enjoys murdering make-believe people.

Rhys can be found at the following locations:

Blog: www.rhysford.com

Facebook: www.facebook.com/rhys.ford.author

X: @Rhys_Ford

Follow me on BookBub

BESTSELLING AUTHOR & TWO-TIME LAMBDA FINALIST

RHYS FORD

BACK IN BLACK

McGINNIS INVESTIGATIONS
BOOK ONE

McGinnis Investigations: Book One

There are eight million stories in the City of Angels but only one man can stumble upon the body of a former client while being chased by a pair of Dobermans and a deranged psycho dressed as a sheep.

That man is Cole McGinnis.

Since his last life-threatening case years ago, McGinnis has married the love of his life, Jae-Min Kim, consulted for the LAPD, and investigated cases as a private detective for hire. Yet nothing could have prepared him for the shocking discovery of a dead, grandmotherly woman at his feet and the cascade of murders that follows, even if he should have been used to it by now.

Now he's back in the dark world of murder and intrigue where every bullet appears to have his name on it and every answer he digs up seems to only create more questions. Hired by the dead woman's husband, McGinnis has to figure out who is behind the crime spree. As if the twisted case of a murdered grandmother isn't complicated enough, Death is knocking on his door, and each time it opens, Death is wearing a new face, leaving McGinnis to wonder who he can actually trust.

www.dreamspinnerpress.com

BEST-SELLING AUTHOR AND LAMBDA FINALIST

RHYS FORD

RAMEN ASSASSIN

RAMEN ASSASSIN: BOOK ONE

Ramen Assassin: Book One

When life gives Kuro Jenkins lemons, he wants to make ponzu to serve at his Los Angeles ramen shop.

Instead he's dodging bullets and wondering how the hell he ended up back in the Black Ops lifestyle he left behind him. After rescuing former child star Trey Bishop from a pair of thugs in the middle of the night, he knows it's time to pick up his gun again. But it seems trouble isn't done with Trey, and Kuro can't quite let go… of either the gun or Trey Bishop.

Trey Bishop never denied his life's downward spiral was his own fault. After a few stints in rehab, he's finally shaken off his Hollywood bad-boy lifestyle but not his reputation. The destruction of his acting career and his relationships goes deep, and no one trusts anything he says, including the LAPD. When two men dragging a dead body spot him on a late-night run and try to murder him, Trey is grateful for the tall, dark, and deadly ramen shop owner he lusts over—not just for rescuing him, but also for believing him.

Now caught in a web of murders and lies, Trey knows someone wants him dead, and the only one on his side is a man with deep, dark secrets. Trey hopes Kuro Jenkins will stick around to see what the future holds for them once the dust settles, but from the looks of things, neither of them may survive to find out.

www.dreamspinnerpress.com

415 ☆ INK • BOOK ONE

Rebel

RHYS FORD

415 Ink: Book One

The hardest thing a rebel can do isn't standing up for something—it's standing up for himself.

Life takes delight in stabbing Gus Scott in the back when he least expects it. After Gus spends years running from his past, present, and the dismal future every social worker predicted for him, karma delivers the one thing Gus could never—would never—turn his back on: a son from a one-night stand he'd had after a devastating breakup a few years ago.

Returning to San Francisco and to 415 Ink, his family's tattoo shop, gave him the perfect shelter to battle his personal demons and get himself together… until the firefighter who'd broken him walked back into Gus's life.

For Rey Montenegro, tattoo artist Gus Scott was an elusive brass ring, a glittering prize he hadn't the strength or flexibility to hold on to. Severing his relationship with the mercurial tattoo artist hurt, but Gus hadn't wanted the kind of domestic life Rey craved, leaving Rey with an aching chasm in his soul.

When Gus's life and world starts to unravel, Rey helps him pick up the pieces, and Gus wonders if that forever Rey wants is more than just a dream.

www.dreamspinnerpress.com

RHYS FORD

SINNER'S GIN

"A raw, sexy read..." — *USA Today*

Sinners Series: Book One

There's a dead man in Miki St. John's vintage Pontiac GTO, and he has no idea how it got there.

After Miki survives the tragic accident that killed his best friend and the other members of their band, Sinner's Gin, all he wants is to hide from the world in the refurbished warehouse he bought before their last tour. But when the man who sexually abused him as a boy is killed and his remains are dumped in Miki's car, Miki fears Death isn't done with him yet.

Kane Morgan, the SFPD inspector renting space in the art co-op next door, initially suspects Miki had a hand in the man's murder, but Kane soon realizes Miki is as much a victim as the man splattered inside the GTO. As the murderer's body count rises, the attraction between Miki and Kane heats up. Neither man knows if they can make a relationship work, but despite Miki's emotional damage, Kane is determined to teach him how to love and be loved — provided, of course, Kane can catch the killer before Miki becomes the murderer's final victim.

www.dreamspinnerpress.com

COLE McGINNIS MYSTERY ROMANCE: ONE

RHYS FORD

DIRTY
KISS

A Cole McGinnis Mystery

Cole Kenjiro McGinnis, ex-cop and PI, is trying to get over the shooting death of his lover when a supposedly routine investigation lands in his lap. Investigating the apparent suicide of a prominent Korean businessman's son proves to be anything but ordinary, especially when it introduces Cole to the dead man's handsome cousin, Kim Jae-Min.

Jae-Min's cousin had a dirty little secret, the kind that Cole has been familiar with all his life and that Jae-Min is still hiding from his family. The investigation leads Cole from tasteful mansions to seedy lover's trysts to Dirty Kiss, the place where the rich and discreet go to indulge in desires their traditional-minded families would rather know nothing about.

It also leads Cole McGinnis into Jae-Min's arms, and that could be a problem. Jae-Min's cousin's death is looking less and less like a suicide, and Jae-Min is looking more and more like a target. Cole has already lost one lover to violence—he's not about to lose Jae-Min too.

www.dreamspinnerpress.com